MATING CHAOS

SHIFTERS OF ASHWOOD FALLS, BOOK 11

LIA DAVIS

CHAPTER ONE

Dane's paws dug into the ground as he ran after his prey. That prey was in the form of two juvenile wolves who moved together as one and knew what the other was about to do.

Brenna and Bryce Baker were a deadly duo and they were just getting started. The teen twins were more powerful than any shifter known. Usually, those with a gift only had one, maybe two abilities. But Brenna and Bryce currently had two each which they could share their abilities with each other. And they were only seventeen and still growing.

A blur of black fur darted in front of him and was gone in a blink.

Fuck Brenna was fast. Dane chased after her

while keeping his senses open for her brother. Bryce was never far away. Darting to his left, Dane followed the teens on pure scent and instincts. The two of them had recently developed the ability to blend into the shadows, making them virtually invisible to the eye.

Working out and training with the Baker twins challenged his wolf and the man to be a better hunter, protector, and Beta for Ashwood Falls. Brenna and Bryce loved it as well. They got to stretch their senses and their powers to see just how far they could push themselves.

A large leopard fell in stride at Dane's side. Alec Andrews. Dane's best friend and the leopard Marshal of Ashwood Falls. Glancing at Alec, Dane jerks his head up toward their right. The big cat grinned and darted in the direction Dane indicated. Alec knew the plan. They were trying to cut them off.

Scanning the woods they were training in, Dane noted that the other junior enforcers were in their positions, running with them and ready to close the twins into a trap. That exercise was one Dane had seen the mutants do almost every time they attacked. However, with the new Big Bad taking over the Onyx Pack and rebuilding it, Dane expected new hunting techniques were needed. What they were, Dane wasn't sure.

They needed to do some scouting and spying on what the new Onyx Alpha was up to. That was something Dane was going to bring up at the next Pack leaders' meeting.

He caught Bryce's scent and took a sharp turn to the left. It didn't take Dane long before he caught up to the teen. His black fur seemed to shimmer under the afternoon sun filtering through the trees.

Just then a leopard jumped out, cutting off Bryce's path. Dane recognized the mix of gold and black fur as being Nigel. He crouched low and showed his teeth to Bryce, letting out a growl.

Bryce growled back, but it sounded more like a taunt. The guys were best friends, forming an instant connection when they met almost a year ago.

A few more wolves and leopards appeared, circling Bryce and closing in. The real test with the exercise was to see how Bryce would get away from being cornered or surrounded. As the group of trainees closed in on Bryce, the wolf paced. Dane sensed that the male was taunting them. When everyone got close enough to form a tight circle around the teen, Bryce vanished.

Fucking teleported.

Just then a snap of a twig had Dane and the others whirled around, bracing for an attack. They were, after all, just outside the protective wards. But all the trainees were strong and knew what to do if attacked.

A young grey wolf stepped out from behind the brush. Dane sighed. Cole Russel. Trouble. Shifting into his human form, Dane addressed the trainees. "Free play for a few."

Dane didn't bother dressing. Nudity was a natural state of being a shifter.

The teens all took off in different directions. Each one knew just how far to go so they weren't caught off guard without someone being able to hear them.

Dane stared down at Cole. "What are you doing here?"

The wolf shook and then he shifted to his nine-year-old human form. Cole lifted his chin. "I want to train with you."

If humans saw them at that moment, they'd think Dane and Cole were part of some weird nudity cult or something. Humans and their insecurities. Shifters had no qualms about being naked in front of each other. It was part of who they were, it was natural.

Dane motioned Cole to follow him. "Does Jas know you are here?"

Cole shook his head. "I've been watching you guys train and I want to be a sentry."

There was a difference in being an Enforcer and a sentry. Sentries were more like the front line of defense. They prowled the edges of the territory looking for breaches and traces of the enemies. They were shifters with a lethal edge to them. A select few could become the Alpha's personal guard. It all depended on the Pack and how their hierarchy was structured. Ashwood Falls didn't have guards on their Alphas because they had pack Marshals and Senior Enforcers.

Dane knew why Cole wanted to be a sentry. His father was one. So it made sense that his sons would fall in his footsteps. "Being a sentry is hard work. It takes a certain skill. And discipline."

"I know." Cole straightened his spine as he walked beside Dane. He and his twin, Kyle, were tall for their age and came to Dane's shoulder. They were still thin and wouldn't bulk up until they hit their teens in a few years. "Jas thinks we're babies. We are not babies."

Cole always used 'we' when talking about what he wanted. He was the dominant twin and always assumed Kyle wanted what he did. Kyle usually went with whatever Cole wanted. Dane thought it was a little unhealthy and so did Jasmine, their sister and guardian.

"I think it's great that *you* want to start training." Dane emphasized the word you, hoping Cole would get the point. He was a smart kid, just didn't act like it most of the time. He was too hot-headed and held in a lot of anger from losing their parents to mutants a few years before. "Have you asked Kyle what he wanted?"

"He does," Cole said instantly. His tone said it wasn't an option.

Dane growled. "You will ask Kyle what he wants." Dane stopped and faced Cole. When the kid met his gaze, Dane added, "Kyle is growing up like you are and will not always want what you want."

Cole rolled his eyes. "You sound like Jasmine."

"She's right."

He grunted and mumbled, "I guess."

They reached the large ash tree where they left their clothes. Cole had left his there too. He dressed and asked, "What are you doing next?"

Dane only put his jeans back on. "We're training in our human forms. It's good for us to know how to protect and fight in both forms."

Cole nodded. "I'm ready."

Brenna came over and grabbed Cole in a headlock even though she was as tall as he was. "Hey, Kiddo."

Cole growled, then laughed and pushed at her to let him go. "Cut it out."

Brenna let him go then rested an arm on his shoulder. "So, Jas finally let you come train?"

Cole glanced at Dane. "Not really."

Dane just shook his head. There was a chance Cole wouldn't like the next exercise and wouldn't come back the following week. Dane was counting on it. "Okay, gather around. We have a guest trainee for the day, so I'm going to go over the rules. The point of this exercise is to build strength and balance. Since the cats are natural climbers, they will stay on the ground and be the hunters. The wolves will be up in the trees. Don't let the hunters find you because they are better climbers."

Alec let out a soft roar to tell the cats to spread out, then he elbowed Dane. "Happy tree climbing."

Dane laughed and met Brenna and Bryce's stares. "Watch out for kiddo."

Brenna nudged Cole. "You ever climbed a tree before?"

Cole puffed out his chest. "Plenty of times."

Bryce laughed. "We'll teach you how to climb without breaking an arm."

The twins directed Cole to the nearest, largest tree and Dane sudden regretted letting the pup join in. If he got hurt, Jasmine would kick Dane's ass. "Don't let him break anything."

Brenna waved him off. "We got this, old man."

The playfulness in her tone made him smile. He jogged to the ash tree and leaped up on the lower branch. He'd been climbing trees with Alec since they were kids. MoonRiver and Ashwood had been allies before the war started and he was glad that his mom, Luna—the current wolf Alpha—continued the alliance after his dad went rogue. So the merger of the Pack was smoother than it would have been if there wasn't already a relationship between the two.

Dane's job was to observe and take note of each wolf, but with Cole there, he couldn't help but to stick close to him.

The kid was a natural sentry. Dane saw it in the way he moved, hunted, and taunted the cats on the ground. He distracted Nigel and another leopard, Steven, while Brenna and Bryce got out of sight. When the two cats got close to capturing Cole, the pup used his speed and strength to evade them at the last moment.

Dane was impressed by how Cole knew just the right time to get away. He also showed other strengths as the training session went on. The kid was ready to start training. Dane bet it would also allow him to expend some pent-up anger and energy.

"That's a wrap." Dane grabbed his shirt from a bush close to the ash tree and slung it over his shoulder.

Within minutes all the teens plus Cole were waiting to make the slow walk back. Brenna, Bryce, and Nigel took the lead and set the pace. Alec and Dane took the rear.

Cole fell into step with Dane and Alec. "Why are we walking so slow?"

"It's to let our bodies and mind cool down and allow time for the adrenaline to leave our system before returning to the den." Dane let the kid process that for a few beats. "I'm impressed with how you did today. You did good."

"Really?" He jumped up and down with excitement.

Dane chuckled. "You're supposed to be cooling down." When Cole returned to walking slow, Dane added, "You can only join as a trainee if Jasmine approves. We need a guardian's consent."

Cole's face went from excited to angry in

moments. "She'll say no. I don't know why I bother." He ran up to the front to walk with Brenna, Bryce, and Nigel.

"It's tough being that age." Alec frowned.

"He still holds a lot of anger and pain from his parents' deaths and takes it out on Jasmine." Dean fisted his hands at his side. The boys, especially Cole, needed a male figure in their lives, someone to look up to. Someone they trusted. Dane was that someone. Jasmine didn't think so.

Alec grunted. "I know how that is personally. Need me to talk to him? Although he looks up to you more than anyone."

Dane watched Cole walk behind the trio at the front with his shoulders sagging as he kicked the ground with each step. "The training program will help him. I'll talk to Jas. Hell, I'll sic Mom on her."

"Yeah, Luna's a good bet to convince her."

"Yeah."

"Rhea and I are meeting Hayden and Crista at Russel's Bar. You should come hang out with us." Alec's tone was void of emotion, but when Dane glanced at him, he saw the mischief in his eyes.

"Yeah, I'll go. But no matchmaker bullshit. I'm perfectly capable of seducing my own mate." Plus

Dane loved the hunt. Each time he approached her, he sensed her walls crumbling. It was about time to pull out the big guns and get a little physical.

Dane was tired of giving her space. It was time to claim his mate.

CHAPTER TWO

*J*asmine exited her office on the second floor of Russel's Bar and glanced over the railing to the growing crowd. It was a few hours away from the after-dinner rush, as she called it. It was about an hour after the average dinner time and when a lot of the Ashwood Pack stops work for the day.

A smile tugged at her lips. She loved the bar. It had been her mother's baby next to her and the twins, Cole and Kyle.

The thought of her nine-year-old brothers made her frown. Kyle had checked in after school, saying he was going to Keegan's to study with the Pack Elder's adopted son, Will. However, Cole hadn't checked in.

She pulled out her cell phone and moved to the stairs when the little hellion stomped up them. He froze at the top of the stairs and locked gazes with her. She eyed him and pressed her lips in a thin line. He was up to something. What else was new?

Waiting for him to spill whatever chaos he'd caused that day, she crossed her arms. He rushed forward and hugged her. The sudden show of affection threw her off at first. She sighed and hugged him back. He was almost eye level with her. The boys were growing up too fast.

Pulling out of the hug she framed his face. "What did you do?"

"Nothing. Honest!" He gave her a kiss on the cheek before moving to their apartment door. "I have homework."

"Your dinner is in the microwave."

He smiled at her and nodded, then ducked into the apartment.

Shaking her head, she descended the stairs. When she reached the bottom floor, she realized that he had totally distracted her from asking where he'd been and why he was late coming home. *The sneaky little demon.*

She did, however, pick up Dane's scent on him so maybe he wasn't in too much trouble. Dane would have punished Cole with manual labor. So that could have been why Cole was late.

Pushing her worry for her brother aside, she moved behind the main bar in the center of the room. Cora was bartending, which was a surprise. Jasmine hadn't put her on the schedule. "Hey, you. What are you doing here?"

Cora was a submissive wolf who'd mated with Torin, a very alpha male wolf Enforcer. Her blue eyes lifted to Jasmine's and she smiled, but Jas sensed nervousness.

"I...I think I'm going into my heat cycle." Cora kept her tone low enough that only Jasmine would hear.

There weren't too many people sitting at the bar where they were. Jasmine smiled and drew the female into a hug. "Is it your first one?"

Cora nodded.

Female shifters went into their heat cycles about every six months or so. Some had theirs more frequently than others. It depended on the female. They all started their cycles when they reached their twenties. Cora was twenty-three.

"Do you want to have babies?"

Cora glanced up and a bright smile formed. "Yes. I'd love to have a large family."

Jasmine cocked her head and stared at Cora, amusement fluttered in her heart. "Why are you here instead of dragging that mate of yours away for the next three or so days?"

Cora drew her brows together and averted her gaze. "What if he doesn't want kids now?'

Leaning against the bar, Jasmine tapped Cora's hand to get her attention. "Have you asked him?"

"No, but..."

"No excuses. Go home strip naked and call your mate to come home to help you with something." Jasmine lifted her brows.

Cora laughed. "That does sound like fun."

Just then she snapped her head up. Jasmine followed her gaze to see Torin entered the bar and head straight for her. Laughing, Jasmine directed Cora around the bar and gave a little nudge toward her mate. "Have fun."

There weren't many things they could hide from their bonded mates. Going into their heat cycle was one of those things. And there was no hiding from them.

Jasmine watched the couple leave with a heavy heart. She longed to be able to claim her mate. In fact, her wolf begged for it. Or at least get a small taste of him and indulge in the mind-blowing sex that came with meeting them.

Yet, she couldn't do it. It wasn't fair to Dane to lock him into a mating she couldn't commit a hundred percent to. Cole and Kyle kept her busy 24/7 and the running the bar was in there somewhere. Her life was a chaotic mess.

His scent slammed into her as soon as the front doors opened, and she suppressed a groan. Lifted her gaze to the entrance, he watched as Hayden and his mate Christa entered with Dane in tow.

His eyes met her instantly and she had to look away. The damn man drove both her and her wolf insane with need.

They took their usual seats that Jasmine called the Enforcers' meeting table located near the south side of the circular bar. She grabbed a pitcher and filled it with their favorite draft, then set it on a tray along with glasses. When the doors opened again and she saw Alec and Rhea enter, Jasmine added two more glasses to the tray.

Blaine, the leopard Alpha, and Cameron, one of the senior Enforcers, usually joined them, but the couple along with their mate Graham was busy with newborn triplets. The thought of the three beautiful little girls who already had their daddies wrapped around their fingers lifted Jasmine's spirits.

She picked up the tray and carried it to the Enforcers table. "Hi. How are you all?"

Hayden and Alec nodded. Rhea said, "It's almost a good day when I don't see either of your brothers in my office."

Jasmine laughed and frowned at the same time. "I know, right? It's weird. Cole came home, late, and instead of giving me shit about it he hugged me. I think he's been possessed by aliens."

"He's starting to mature." Rhea poured herself a beer then handed the pitcher to Alec.

"Yeah, he's a good kid, just needs something to focus on." Alec set the pitcher in the middle of the table and picked up the food menu. "Have you considered letting them start the junior Enforcer trainee group? We're starting new classes in about a month."

Jasmine shook her head. "They're too young." She met Dane's stare and saw something she didn't recognize. "Plus they don't have to be Enforcers just because Dad was."

A lump formed in her throat, but she swallowed it. Hayden took the menu from Alec while he was reading it. "Dane, Tanner, and I started the day after our first shift."

Yeah, because you had a sadist as a father. The thought popped in her mind and she regretted the negativity of it. The Raines brothers were not like Royce. They were strong, compassionate males. "How much of that was your choice?"

Hayden shrugged, but Dane answered. "It gave us something to focus on."

"Becoming stronger enough to protect our mom, pushed us to be the best." The steal in Hayden's voice told Jasmine the brothers still held resentment for their dead father.

She sighed. "I'll think about. They just need to survive middle school."

Christa spoke up, changing the subject. Jasmine was thankful. "Hey, Rhea and Ana are planning a girls' night."

Rhea perked up. "Ana and I want to get Cameron out of the house. So Shay said she'd pry the female from those babies for a few hours. Want to come?"

"Where too?" A night out sounded fun.

"We haven't decided. Our Alpha mates don't think we should leave the den." Rhea rolled her eyes.

Jasmine laughed. Rhea had revealed to the whole

Pack that she was a born Hunter. The female that ran the nursery and the school was just as powerful as the Alphas. However, she still kept her powers behind a wall and was content with being just the Pack's head den mother.

"But you'll be there. And Ana. And Sable?" Jasmine glanced a the alpha males at the table.

Rhea frowned. "With Sable being pregnant, Jared put his foot down. So we might have to compromise and let some of them go with us."

"They don't have to hang out with us. They can just follow like a group of growly stalkers." Jasmine scrunched her face. "But seriously, I'm good with just hanging out with friends. We don't do it nearly enough. Things have been so tense for so long."

Christa nodded. "You're right."

"We'll let you know when we work out the deets, "Rhea added.

Jasmine heard her name and turned to see Myles, her night shift cook, stick his head out from the back. Turning back to the table, she said, "I'll be back. This is Judy's table so when you're ready to order, just shout for her."

She ducked into the kitchen. "What is it?"

"We're out of wings."

She frowned. "How are we out of wings?"

"Shipment was supposed to come in this morning, and it didn't. Instead, we got double the salmon."

Damn. "Okay, it's not the end of the world. I'll give them a call to see what's up. Do you have any ideas for a special we can offer instead?"

Myles was taking culinary classes and loved to encourage his creativity. He smiled. "I could do something with the extra salmon we got and do boneless wings using the chicken breast we have or something."

"Sounds great. When you figure it out, let Judy know so she can let the staff know and update the board with the nightly specials." Jasmine walked out of the kitchen and jumped at the sight of Dane standing in the short hallway.

She eyed him suspiciously. "What?"

He stepped closer, pinning her to the wall. Her heartbeat increased and fought the urge to touch him. When he lowered his head to hers, she almost groaned. His woodsy scent enveloped her, wetting her panties. Damn him.

"Have dinner with me tomorrow night." His voice was thick with desire and she realized at that moment he was tired of waiting on her.

"I can't. I have to make sure the boys do their

homework and I'm working." It was the truth even though it sounds like excuses.

"Then I'll bring you takeout at your place."

She snorted. "We live in the mountains. The closest take out is an hour drive."

"I'll bring you cold take out and we can warm it up."

Gods help her. She shook her head, and he closed the small gap between them, pressing his body to hers. "I can come up tonight and bake you a cake, naked."

The image of his naked body flashed in her mind and she gripped his shirt in her hands. She breathed in his scent. It was so hard to push him away when she wanted him so bad. "Why are you doing this?"

"Because you are mine." He nuzzled her neck and she whimpered.

"I can't..."

He bit down on her ear, stopping her words. Then he lifted his head to stare into her eyes. "I know what I'm getting into. Those boys look up to me and know one day you and I will be mated. Putting it off is only make me want you more."

Stubborn male. The fact that she was growing tired of running concerned her. "Fine." She poked him in the chest. "Come up for desert, but I'll be in my pajamas with my hair down and messy. I want to date before we bond. Take me out, which most cases will include the boys so you can see exactly what you are signing up for."

He captured her mouth in a searing, raw kiss. Passion exploded in her mind and her core. Threading her fingers into his hair, she pulled him closer, deepening the kiss. His tongue dipped inside her mouth and tangled with hers. He tasted of beer and male.

With her free hand, she slid it underneath his shirt so she could feel his heated skin. Damn him. He made her want things that were impossible.

Dane broke the kiss and stared down at her. "I'll see you in a couple of hours."

She nodded. When he walked away, she sagged against the wall, her heart hammering inside her. After a few moments, she escaped the bar to her apartment on the second floor. There was no way she could face him again in public that night.

She needed a cold shower and a drink.

CHAPTER THREE

Faelin wasn't like other mutants. He was stronger, able to shift between his human and wolf forms, and he remembers his life before Felix Darwin injected him with the serum that made him who he was.

However, Faelin wasn't a mutant, exactly. He was something other, more powerful than the brainless shells of assassins Felix raised.

And he was going to finish what his father started.

He dipped his fingers into the water of the scrying bowl and moved them in circular motions, swirling the water in a counterclockwise direction. "Show me the heart of Ashwood Falls."

The picture formed almost instantly of the

leopard Alpha, Blaine with his two mates and three newborn daughters. The happy family was playing with the three cubs and smiling like they deserved their little sense of peace. It wouldn't last for long.

The image shifted to the second Alpha, a female wolf, Luna Raines. Her dark curly red hair cascaded around the shoulders as she sat in an open yard of the nursery with a bunch of cubs and pups around her, imitating her slow moments. Faelin had seen others do what they were doing. Yoga, he thought it was called. Sable and Ana used to do it. Sable said it helped with centering the inter beast and with focus.

The thought of Sable made him frown. She didn't even recognize him during their brief encounter a few weeks before when she stole the kids from him. In fact, she stared at him as if she was looking at a complete stranger.

"Show me Sable." The water rippled and the image flashed to Sable. She was with Ana and they were out for a run. Alone.

Perfect.

Using the visual he got from the scrying bowl, he teleported to the location where Sable and Ana were. He materialized next to a large ash tree and watched the females for a little while. But his presence didn't go unnoticed. Ana stopped and moved in front of Sable, protectively.

Sable placed a hand on her sister's arm. "Not helpless," she said playfully to Ana before turning deadly serious. "Who's there?"

Faelin stepped out from his hiding place and inclined his head to his sisters. "Good evening."

The females fell into a defensive stance. Ana snarled, "What are you doing here?"

"How did you get inside the wards?" Sable glared at him, her lips pressed into a thin line as her magic swirled inside her teal eyes.

Faelin lifted one shoulder. "Your wards cannot keep me out. Besides, I'm not here to harm you." *This time.* He kept those two words to himself. "You don't remember me." he began to circle them.

They followed him, not giving him their backs. Smart females.

Sable straightened. "Why don't you refresh our memories?"

His lips lifted in a slow smile. "I was Felix's beta before you became old enough to take the job."

Focusing on her, he let his true human appearance show through his normal mutated state. Sable frowned, then her features morphed to recognition. "Unax?"

He bowed his head. "I don't go by that name anymore. Father gave me that name. My mother named me Faelin."

Sable glanced at Ana then back to him while crossing her arms. "What do you want?"

"Is that any way to greet your brother?" He watched her as she fisted her hands at her side and glared at him. She was most likely calculating ways to kill him. It was Sable he was dealing with, after all.

She could pretend she left Onyx behind, but she was still Felix and Savannah's daughter. Lethal magic flowed in her veins. And Faelin needed her on his side.

"You are not my brother." Sable stepped forward. The air around him tingled with her power. The earth under his feet trembled and he jerked his gaze to Ana, the elemental.

Sable spoke again, drew his attention back to her. "If you were Felix's son, you'd be the beta and not me. Felix may have been insane but he stuck to Pack hierarchy. Plus he would have told me." A flash of acknowledgment brightened her features. She straightened and cocked her head to the side. "I remember now. Unax."

He blanched at the name. He hated to be called Unax. The bastard Royce Raines used his name only when he was being punished. Faelin was never strong enough or fast enough for Royce, who was the Onyx Marshal at the time, as well as the Alpha of MoonRiver. How the male had lived a double life, Faelin wasn't sure, but the male pulled it off until his mate found out and killed him for it.

"You aren't Felix's son." Sable continued. "You were created in the labs and your mother was forced to carry the baby via artificial insemination. But it was not Felix's sperm that impregnated your mother. It was Royce's."

Faelin growled and jumped back. No. That couldn't be true. "You lie."

She smiled wickedly. "Why would I do that?" Her teal eyes flashed darker as her leopard looked out at him. "But I'm not sure if you get your power from Royce or from the serum Felix injected you with. There could be a small chance Savannah played a part in it."

She was lying. She had to be. Well not about his powers. Although he didn't get them from the mutant serum. That was a secret he'd keep to himself for now.

The rustling of leaves made him snap his head to the right. He met the lethal stares of Sable's mate Jared, Ana's mate, Kieran, and one of Ashwood's sentries, Tanner. It was Tanner who Faelin focused on.

The youngest Raines son snarled as he stepped closer. Kieran held up his hand to stop the hot-headed sentry. "You're not welcomed here. We don't want another war, but if you start one we'll finish it."

Oh, Faelin had no doubt Kieran believed they could win a war against him. That arrogant misplaced pride was going to be their downfall. He'd gone there to see if there was any way to persuade Sable into joining him. To his surprise, she had indeed changed her alliance. She wasn't the same lethal Beta she once was.

Locking gazes with Kieran, Faelin curled his upper lip. "We'll see who comes out the victor."

Faelin ported to his apartment inside the mountain that once was the Onyx den. His thoughts swirled around what Sable said. Royce Raines was his father. The cruel bastard had made Faelin's life a living hell after he was injected with the serum. Royce pushed him to be the meanest, biggest, and strongest.

Each training session and each punishment fueled Faelin's desire to kill the asshole. He'd plotted how he'd make Royce's death slow and painful, stretch it out for as long as Faelin had to endure every beating and punishment Royce put him through.

Luna Raines took away Faelin's right to make Royce suffer. He didn't deserve a quiet death.

"Easton!"

Within moments of yelling for his Beta, the male appeared in his doorway. "Yes?"

"I need to know everything you can gather up about Luna Raines and her sons." Faelin would use their abilities and weaknesses against them and make them pay for taking away his right to seek revenge on the bastard who made him the monster he'd become.

CHAPTER FOUR

Dane knocked on Jasmine's apartment door. The bar down below was still booming and he wondered how she got any sleep with the bar open until 2:00 a.m. However, he knew she stayed up pretty late. Most of the time she worked the bar until it closed.

The door opened and Kyle frowned at him. His hair was a little longer than Cole's, making it easy to tell the twins apart. Although Dane could tell who was who by their scent and their wolves. Cole was more alpha than Kyle.

"Jas and I have a date." Dane lifted his brows at the kid.

Kyle scrunched his face up. "I don't need the details." He stepped aside and Dane entered the spacious apartment. "Jas is in the shower. She'll be out in a few."

Just then Cole entered the living room from the hallway. He gave Dane a nod in greeting. "What's up?"

Kyle rolled his eyes. "Date night," he muttered as he sat on the sofa and picked up his math book.

Cole's features darkened briefly before he forced a smile and crossed the room to the kitchen. "Cool."

Dane studied the kid for several long moments. Cole was hard to read sometimes. The kid held in a lot of anger and pain. Jasmine had been trying to get him to go see Nevan—the human psychiatrist that was mated to Dani, the leopard Healer. Nevan grew up with a puma as a stepmom and three puma brothers. Shifters were not new to the human. In fact, Nevan even acted like a cat most of the time.

Dane decided to ignore Cole's reaction to him being there for now. The kid knew better than to push Dane's buttons. As the Pack Beta, Dane held rank over him and Jasmine. Sitting on the sofa with Kyle, Dane pointed at the book. "Math was my worse subject."

Cole laughed. "Kyle loves it."

Kyle shrugged. Dane always tried to get Kyle to answer his own questions. However, if Cole was around, he always answered for his twin. Ignoring, Cole's attempts to annoy him, because the kid knew that it got under his skin how Cole dominated his brother, Dane picked up the remote and motioned to the TV, directing his question to Kyle. "Do you mind if I change this?"

There was a race on, but it was recorded from the weekend before. Dane had watched it over Hayden's house.

Kyle shook his head, but Cole said, "He just has it on for noise."

"Are you finished with your homework, Cole?" Dane flipped through the guide to see what was on.

Cole sat his glass on the counter hard and stormed down the hall. Moments later his bedroom door slammed shut.

Glancing at Kyle, Dane asked, "Have you ever thought about joining the junior enforcers training classes?"

Kyle shrugged. "Jas won't let us."

"But have you thought about it?"

A sigh slipped from his lips and he closed his math book and set it on the coffee table. "Yes. Although I'm not sure I want to be an Enforcer or a sentry. That's more Cole's thing. But the training classes will be good to strengthen my abilities and senses."

"I was seven when I started training."

Kyle glanced at him, his brows dipping. "Did you...have a choice?"

Dane knew what he was asking. "Yes and no. As the Alpha's sons, my brothers and I would go through the training, after all, we were the future Pack leaders. It made us stronger, faster, and helped us learn to control the feral part of us that came from our father."

That feral part lurked behind their wolves, taunting and tempting them to hunt and kill. Hayden and Dane had learned to block it, to not give in to that side. But Tanner struggled with it at times.

"How do you control that side? The anger. The darkness."

Dane met Kyle's stare. He'd always sensed a power hidden inside the twins. It wasn't magick like Blaine's teleporting or what Brenna and Bryce carry within. It was different. Their father, Jerome, had the same inner strength. It was what made him a damn good Enforcer.

"The training helped, but mostly it was my mom who taught us to accept it and use it to direct it to fight for our Pack. Does that make sense?" Dane watched Kyle as his features softened.

"I've been taking Luna's yoga classes in the mornings. It's helping. I wish Cole would take them." Kyle glanced at the hallway.

Dane's body reacted to hearing and scenting Jasmine as she opened her bedroom door.

"Cole! Stop slamming the damned door!" A few minutes after yelling at Cole, Jasmine entered the living room and met his stare. She frowned and narrowed her gaze. "What did you say to him that pissed him off? I don't need to deal with his attitude tonight."

Dane racked his gaze over her. Her long curly brown hair was wet and flowed over her shoulders and down her back. She wore a purple tank top and a pair of shorts with paw prints on them. A picture of beauty and sensual perfection. His mate. Suppressing a growl, he said, "I asked him if he had homework after he repeatedly answered questions directed at Kyle."

"Huh." Jasmine moved to the kitchen and grabbed a bottle of water before going to the other side of the sofa next to Kyle. She picked up his homework. "This is great. Are you getting it now?"

Kyle nodded. "Yeah. Thanks for your help."

Jasmine cupped his cheek and kissed his forehead. "I'm always here for you and Cole."

Kyle leaned into her and hugged her. "We know." He stood and collected his books, then gave Dane a short nod. "Night."

When Kyle left the room, Jasmine sighed. "I don't know when they got so tall."

He slid across the sofa and drew her into his arms. She tensed at first, then settled against him, placing a hand on his chest as she curled into him. His wolf pressed up against his skin, wanting to feel her wolf.

Soon. He told his wolf. They would be mated and their wolves would be connected as well.

"They are growing up. Which is why now is the perfect time for them to start training." When she stiffened and started to pull away from him, he tightened his arms around her. "I know how you feel. I also know from personal experience how difficult it is to deal with loss and all that power they carry around. I'd prefer them to release it and learn to control it during a controlled setting."

"I hear you. And you're right. I just don't want them to get hurt or feel like they don't have a choice."

Dane pressed his lips to her forehead and

inhaled her rose water scent. "I need you to keep an open mind and not go yell at Cole."

She sat up and glared at him. "Why? What did he do?"

Dane frowned. "He showed up at the junior enforcer training today." He paused briefly before adding, "And I let him participate."

"What? Did he get hurt?"

Dane chuckled. "He did really well. He partnered up with Brenna and was able to keep up with her. She might want him to partner with for training from now on because the two of them gave Bryce and Nigel the runaround. It was awesome to watch."

Jasmine shook her head. "I'm not sure I'm ready for this. I keep telling myself that they are too young. That they need time to be kids."

"The war had changed us all. Cole and Kyle stopped being kids when your parents were murdered." He leaned in and kissed her lips softly. "It's time to let them grow up. They don't have to be Enforcers if they don't want. But the training is good for them. I think Mom is talking to Rhea about adding it to the curriculum for third-graders and up."

"I'll think about it." Sadness clouded her features. "I don't want to lose them. I can't lose them."

He hugged her close, feeling how tired she was, not just physically, but emotionally too. He understood her fear. Mutants had killed her parents. "You won't lose them. I won't allow it. Mom won't allow it."

"Thank you."

They fell silent for a few and he flipped through the TV channels until he came across a romantic comedy movie and Jasmine said to leave it. About three quarters through the movie Jasmine fell asleep. Her soft snores were adorable.

After turning the TV off, he carried her to bed then made sure the apartment was secure and lights off before returning to her bed. He stripped down to his boxer briefs and slipped under the covers with her.

After kissing her cheek, he curled around her from behind. "Goodnight, Mate."

CHAPTER FIVE

*J*asmine woke curled up against Dane. A smile lifted her lips as she watched the rise and fall of his chest as he slept. Her mate.

It felt amazing to wake up in his arms. She reached up and ran her fingers through his hair, then traced her fingers down his cheek. When she reached his lips, he nipped at them, startling her.

He rolled until his body pinned hers to the bed and wedged her thighs part. A groan stuck in her throat as he rolled his hips, pressing his hard cock into her core. He lowered his mouth to press against her skin and trailed feather-like kisses down her stomach. He tore her shorts off and pushed her legs up to settle her thighs over his shoulders. Then he covered her pussy with his mouth. She bucked at the wild sensations running through her, then moaned as his tongue teased the bundle of nerves.

She fisted her hands in his hair and moved her hips in time with each of his licks. A gasp escaped her when he slid a finger inside her. A rush of emotions mixed with intense pleasure burned through her. Dane slid another finger inside her, drawing a groan from her. She bucked her hips, let go of his hair to fist the sheets, and tried to crawl backward to break the contact, if for only a moment. Dane grabbed her hips, holding her in place.

Gods, the man was going to kill her with the desire he ignited inside her. Heat covered her body, and she didn't know how much more of this slow, pleasurable torture she could take.

He pumped his fingers in and out faster and harder until she screamed his name as an orgasm tore through her.

Panting and unable to move, she watched as Dane withdrew his fingers and crawled up her body, a grin on his face.

She rolled her eyes and tried not to smile. That was too hard, especially when she'd just had the best orgasm ever. "I can't move. I'm broken, and it's all your fault."

He chuckled and swiped his tongue over a nipple, drawing another moan from her. "Broken, huh? I could have my way with you, and you can't do anything about it."

Good gods, he didn't know just how true that was.

He continued his slow, graceful crawl up her torso until his face was level with hers. She cupped his face and pulled him down for a kiss. He growled, which did nothing but excite her even more.

She circled her ankles around the backs of his thighs and tugged him closer until his erection pressed into her through his boxers. She scowled. "Boxers. Off."

He leaned down to place his lips on her ear and whispered, "Say please."

Her heart thumped faster, and heat pooled between her legs. She fought with her wolf for a few moments, wanting to be a little defiant. Finally losing to her submissive nature, she groaned out her reply. "Please."

His answer was a devilish smirk that sent a shiver through her. He tore his boxers off and settled between her legs. Then he pressed his lips to hers in a brief, but soft kiss as he cradled her head between his hands.

He rolled his hips forward and entered her with a quick thrust. A wildfire of sensation raced inside her as well as over her skin. Dane's scent intensified, and she inhaled it, loving everything about it, about this male.

She moved against him as he thrust into her over and over as the pleasure built until she was consumed by it, unable to think about anything but the way Dane was loving her.

"Come for me."

His command was husky and low. Her body obeyed and the orgasm exploded through her. She bit his shoulder to keep from screaming and alerting the boys.

Dane tensed right before his own release slammed into him.

JASMINE POURED a cup of coffee as Dane came up behind her, snaking his arms around her and kissed her neck. She let a soft groan.

"Get a room," Kyle said as he came into the kitchen and grabbed a glass from the cabinet.

Jasmine laughed and pointed to the table. "Breakfast is ready."

Kyle grabbed the juice from the fridge and carried it to the table. "This looks great. Did Dane cook?"

"Hey." Jasmine turned to face Kyle, smiling. She met Dane's amused gaze. "I can cook."

She knew Kyle was teasing her. If Cole was in there he'd get them all going on taunts and name calling. All in fun. Where was Cole?

As soon as she asked the question, he appeared from the hallway. He glanced at Dane and his lips twitched. "You still here?"

"Yep. Get used to it, Kid." Dane smirked and sat at the table between the boys.

The sight of Dane inserted into her little family warmed her heart and soul. Probably a little more than she wanted. Times like that morning where the boys were pleasant and playful gave her hope that things would get better. The chaos that surrounds them will settle down. And one day they'd learn to live as a family instead of three people just trying to survive their own pain.

She took her cup of coffee and sat at the table. As

she picked up her fork, she said, "Dane told me you joined the training yesterday."

Cole dropped his fork and sat back in his chair, crossing his arms. "And?"

Her wolf snarled in her head. But she pushed back the urge to snap at Cole for being disrespectful. In a calm tone, she said, "He said you did well and actually kept up with Brenna, which is something because she's pretty strong and fast."

Cole puffed out his chest and picked up his fork. His defensiveness melted away. "She's nice and moves kind of like a cat. It's weird."

Jasmine didn't know a lot about the Baker twins, but she knew they spent a lot of time hiding and running from Shield—a human run militant group that hunted down shifters—and mutants. That could be the need to learn to be as silent and light on their feet as possible, which would explain why two wolf shifters would move like cats, as Cole put it. "Why don't you ask her how she moves like that? Maybe, she'd teach you some tricks."

Cole perked up. "You're okay with us training?"

"I've slept on it and agree with Dane that it would benefit you both." She looked at Kyle and added, "It's your choice. Individual choices." She narrowed her gaze at Cole.

"Yeah, I get it. Kyle has different interests. I'm trying to not push him." Cole frowned.

Dane added, "You know, even though the Baker twins have the bond they do, they have different interests as well."

Cole seemed to think about it as he finished his breakfast. Jasmine took that time to put down some ground rules. "You two can join the enforcer training, but your grades have to stay up. And no more getting into trouble. I get a call about you pulling a stupid prank or talking back to your teachers or anything, you don't train."

Dane nodded, agreeing with her. "Training is not all fun and games. It's about discipline, control, and balance. Plus Cameron will be taking over classes. If you think Alec and I are hard asses, you're going to wish you were mauled by a bear when Cameron gets done with you."

Jasmine smiled, holding in her giggle. Cameron was tough and would be tougher since she had the triplets. Her maternal instincts would be heightened. She'll keep Cole in line for sure.

Cole jumped up and took his plate to the sink. "We'll work hard. Promise. No more trouble."

Jasmine hoped so, but she wondered how long

that positive attitude would last. "You start by being on time for school for once."

Cole collected his and Kyle's backpacks from the living room. After Kyle put his plate in the sink, he met his brother at the door, taking his bag from Cole.

Dane pointed at them. "Be sure to go straight to class. You don't want me to walk you to class and embarrass you. Ask Luna what she did to me and my brothers when we skipped school once."

Cole frowned and Kyle looked worried as they left for school.

Dane stood and collected the dishes and carried them to the sink. Then he proceeded to wash them.

"I have a dishwasher." She joined him at the sink and started drying. "What did Luna do?"

A sexy smile formed and he chuckled. "Hayden and I skipped school one time and she walked us to class in the most ridiculous looking pajamas she could find with huge bunny slippers. But that wasn't the bad part. She'd make sure to walk us into the classroom and fuss at us about not knowing directions enough to walk to school. Then she'd make up an embarrassing medical issue like a rash on our butts or other parts."

Jasmine burst out laughing. "I love your mother. I will need to go get parenting tips from her."

He leaned in her and pressed his lips to hers. "What did you want to do today?"

"I have work. It's payroll day. Plus I need to make the schedule for the next two weeks." The idea of spending the day with him sounded relaxing.

His wolf flashed in his blue-green gaze. "Yeah. I should check in at the office. Sable had a run in with Faelin yesterday."

"Oh? Is she okay?"

Dane worked his jaw. "Yeah. She and Ana were out on a run inside the wards. The bastard just teleported in like he was allowed to."

"What? How?" Fear burned Jasmine's insides. If the new Alpha of Onyx could get through Ashwood's protective barriers, then none of them were safe.

Dane framed her face. "He got in because his intensions were not threatening. Mom said we'll have to alter the wards to be more specific on who to keep out. Not sure how they will manage that."

Nodding, she wrapped her arms around Dane and hugged him close. The steady *thump*, *thump* of his heart soothed her. "Keep me updated so I don't worry myself sick."

"I will." Dane's phone chimed and he glanced at

it. "Tanner texted. Mom and Blaine called a meeting."

Jasmine pulled back but Dane captured her mouth in a searing kiss. "I'll pick you up this afternoon and we'll go on a proper date."

CHAPTER SIX

Dane walked into the home of Blaine and his two mates, the leopard Alpha's home. It was where they had always held meetings since merging the two packs. The former Ashwood Alpha, Keegan used to live in the house until he mated with the Pack Scribe, Addyson, and turned over the Alpha power to Blaine.

As he moved further into the living room, he spotted his mom holding two of the triplets. He smiled. If Luna could, she'd hold all three at once. She glanced up at him and offered a small smile. "Aren't they beautiful?"

"They are." He moved to Cameron and gave her a hug. "Like their mom."

She hugged him back. "And this mama is glad to be back at work."

Sable and Ana entered the house a few moments later and Dane drifted back to sit on a bar stool at the kitchen island with Alec and Travis. Alec had his laptop open. He shook his head and let out a soft growl. "The sensors in that area didn't even pick up the bastard's presence."

That was interesting. The wards were built on magic and technology that was supposed to keep outsiders out. Especially if they wished to do them harm. So how did Faelin get in without setting off the alarms? But he'd hold his questions until Sable briefed everyone on what happened. His mom had gave him limited information the day before.

Luna motioned to Sable. "This is your meeting so go for it."

Sable nodded. "Ana and I were on our afternoon run when Faelin approached us. Oddly enough, he didn't come to attack. He wanted to talk, I guess. Maybe he hoped that I'd just hand over information or join his side? Who knows, the male is psycho." Frowning she glanced at Blaine, then Luna.

Blaine sat on the sofa next Luna and tried to take back one of his daughters. Luna wasn't giving up either of the girls. Giving up, Blaine said, "He's arrogant enough to believe that you would just join him."

Sable nodded. "Yeah, I agree. As I was talking to him, I remembered where I know him. He is not related to me as we speculated. He doesn't get his power from Savannah. I'd feel it, which I didn't." She paused and meet Luna's stare.

Luna gave them a slight nod. "Go ahead, tell them."

"Felix didn't create Fealin. Royce did."

Shock froze Dane's insides and he stared at Sable. "What do you mean?"

"Before I was born, Felix would use his own DNA and sperm to create mutants. He would get a female to carry the baby, then take it from her and raise the child to be an assassin. When they reached adulthood, he'd inject them with the serum." Sable moved to a chair and sat down, putting her head in her hands. "Royce fathered two of the children. One didn't make it past three years old. The second was born to a witch who ran off with the child and raised him until Royce tracked her down and killed her."

Fealin was Dane's brother? Half brother and falling in his rouge of a father's footsteps. "Are you sure of this?"

Sable nodded and lifted her gaze to his. "Yeah.

Fealin was known as Unax and was the Beta of Onyx until I became of age to take the position. Felix was very thorough in his training, making sure I knew about who everyone was. He made it clear that Unax...Faelin was Royce's bastard."

The room was silent for several minutes. Then Sable added, "I sensed that he might be putting his sights on Luna. He was surprised when I told him that Royce was his father, so he'll be wanting to find out if I lied or not."

Dane shook his head, trying to process the news. Then the realization hit him that Royce was on the wrong side of the war before he mated Luna. There was telling how many other children he had before then.

"We need to fix the weakness in the wards and make sure Faelin can't get inside again." Dane steeled his voice and met his mom's stare. Her green depths were a mix of sadness and anger.

Even from the grave Royce was hurting her. Now his bastard son was picking up where he left off.

Blaine broke the silence. "We'll go on with normal daily activities. I'll get together with Kieran about sending out our own scouts and spies to gather information about Faelin and see what he is up to."

"I'll talk to Rhea too. Even though she doesn't want to, I think she needs to be brought in on these meetings so she's ready when and if we need her." Alec frowned and pulled out his phone and sent a text.

Rhea was a born Hunter with abilities so deadly she'd kept it a secret from the Pack until Faelin kidnapped the kids almost a month ago. Dane didn't blame her for wanting to keep her powers on the down low. His own power was something he didn't voluntarily tell people. It was unsettling to most when they find out someone can call the dead and use them as your personal army.

Then there was the whole empathy on steroids thing.

Just then little Max entered the living room and looked around, glancing at each face until he found Luna. He walked to her, crawled up on the sofa next to her and kissed his sisters on their foreheads.

Speaking of empathy, Max was already showing strong healer abilities and his empathy was something they were all watching. If it turned out to be anything like Dane's abilities, the toddler would need to start training soon.

Blaine drew everyone's attention away from the

kids by saying, "One thing we know is that Faelin needs to rebuild the Onyx den and grow his army."

Sable nodded. "Yeah, but I get the feeling he is not continuing with the mutants. However, we can't rule that out. He's not all sane but he's smart. That's a bad combo."

Sure the fuck was. Felix was crazy, but he wasn't all that smart. He depended on others to create the serum and he ruled by controlling his people.

"What about the Rebels and Shield?" Dane asked.

Hayden answered. "Shield was taken down when Lance was killed. Christa is still watching out for it to start back up. From what she can find out, those who supported Lance had joined the Rebel groups."

"I still have a contact with the Rebel group that is working with the shifter communities. I can reach out to her and check on things." Sable glanced from Blaine to Luna.

Blaine gave her a single nod. "That would be good. At least we'd know if we have to deal with them as well." He paused for a few moments. "If there isn't anything else we need to discuss since we're all here, then this meeting is done. I'll stop by

Dad's today and give him an update. Not sure why he wasn't here this morning."

Sable grinned. "You might want to call first. Will has been staying at our house for the last two days."

Ana laughed. "I offered Will to stay with Kieran and me, but he like Jared for some reason."

Blaine frowned. "Why...oh, never mind. I'll call him later then."

There were very few things that would keep Keegan from attending a Pack meeting. His mate going through her heat cycle would be high on that list. That was what it sounded like. Especially if Will was staying with Sable and Jared.

The meeting broke apart and Dane checked the time. It was too early to pull Jasmine away from her work so he walked the few blocks to the center of town where the medical center and office buildings were. He had a stack of paperwork waiting on him, plus he had to check the Pack's stock portfolio.

When he entered his office Bryce was sitting in one of the chairs playing a game on his phone. Raising a brow, Dane said, "Are you in trouble?"

Bryce shook his head. "I asked to be excused from school today."

"And you thought hanging out with me would be

fun?" Dane sat behind his desk and watched the teen.

Bryce put his phone away and met Dane's gaze. A storm of emotions brewed in his blue depths. Dane's empathy picked up on each emotion: Fear, anger, happiness, and confusion. After a few moments, Bryce said, "I saw my dad."

Frowning, Dane sat back in his and pointed to the door. "Close the door, please."

Bryce did as he was asked but didn't sit back down. Before the teen said anything or asked questions, Dane said, "Did you call to your dad's spirit?"

"I don't think so."

"Were you thinking of him right before you saw him?"

Bryce shook his head. "No. When I mentioned it to Christa this morning Hayden said to come to talk with you."

"Did he say why?"

"No, but I assumed it was because you are the ghost expert in the Pack."

Dane chuckled. "Not the expert." He paused, looking for the right words to explain what he can do. "Some people are sensitive to energies and it's not uncommon for shifters to see ghosts. With the number of abilities that you and

Brenna are showing, I understand why Hayden told you to come to me. I have a gift, well more than one, that I don't use or broadcast that I have them."

"Why?"

Dane frowned. "They're just not very useful in protecting the pack. One of those powers is the ability to call to the dead. I can raise the dead for a certain amount of time and call to ghosts that maybe in the area. Again, not useful and not something I like to do."

Bryce stared at him for a long moment. "Is that one or two gifts?"

"One. My other is empathy strong enough to control another's emotions." Dane considered Bryce for a little while. "I don't think you have the ability to call to the dead, because you said you weren't thinking of your father."

"I've sensed a presence for a few days. It was like someone was watching me. Brenna said she did too. But this morning, I stepped out of my room and there he was, standing in the hallway." Bryce's eyes watered and Dane felt his sorrow flow from him in waves.

"What do you want to do about it?"

Bryce shrugged and averted his gaze. "I just don't

know why he suddenly showed up. How long has he been watching us?"

"If he shows again today, ask him. If he doesn't, then tomorrow you, Brenna, and I will go to the Pack circle and I'll call him out so you two can ask your questions." Dane wanted to talk with Christa about the twin's father and what he was dealing with before called the ghost to have a chat with him.

Bryce glanced at the closed office door. "Can you control ghosts when you call them?"

"No. Which is why I'll be talking with your aunt first."

"Yeah, okay." Bryce stood just as Hayden entered the office.

Hayden glanced from Dane to Bryce. "You okay?"

Bryce nodded. "I'm going to hang out with Christa."

When Hayden nodded the teen made his escape. Then Hayden met Dane's gaze with a raised brow. Dane fired up his computer. While it was starting up he shuffled through the stack of papers on his desk. He had to get the financials to his Mom and Blaine by the end of the week.

Hayden sat in the chair Bryce was in moments ago. "Does he have the same gift as you?"

"No. I think Rick showed up for a reason. Bryce said he's been feeling like someone was watching him for a while. When I'm done here I'll go talk to Christa and get more information on Rick. I don't want to call him to play Q&A with his kids if he's hostile." Dane clicked on the bookmark for the Ashwood Falls stock portfolio.

Hayden stared at him for several moments. "What's going on with you?"

"Nothing, why?"

A twisted grin formed on his brother's face. "You are not usually in the office this early."

Meeting his big brother's assumed gaze. "If you must know, nosey-ass. I have a date with Jasmine this afternoon and tonight."

"About time." Hayden laughed. "Tanner thinks Mom had another vision. He says she's a little weirded out and when he asks her about it she says it's nothing. "

That was odd. Usual his mom would share her visions with the Alphas and the Enforcers to ensure the Pack was protected. As far as Dane knew, his mom's visions were usually about an attack on the den or other fatal events.

"What do you think it is?"

Hayden shrugged. "Not sure, but you know Mom. She'll deal with her own problems her way."

Dane's wolf snarled. Yeah, he knew. Luna was a strong, independent, stubborn female. If her life was in danger, she wouldn't get her sons involved. "We'll keep an eye on her. She doesn't go anyway without a sentry."

"Way ahead of you." Hayden stood and stretched. "Just wanted to give you a heads up."

"Thanks."

When Hayden moved to the door, he said, "Enjoy your date."

Dane planned on it. Jas was his and he'd do whatever it took to convince her to give into the mating.

CHAPTER SEVEN

*J*asmine was making the final adjustments to the schedule when Dane knocked on her office door. Lifting her gaze to meet his, she couldn't stop the smile from forming. He wore the same form-fitting t-shirt he did that morning and the low-waisted faded blue jeans. Damn the male was hot.

Her wolf agreed with that assessment, ready to claim him in every way possible.

Averting her gaze and feeling her cheeks heat, she closed out of her computer software, then shut it down. "How was the meeting?"

"Informative." A darkness passed through his blue-green gaze.

"What is it?" Fear flared hot in her belly.

Dane frowned and crossed the room to her in a flash. He crouched down by her chair and framed her face. "The den is not in danger." he sighed and pressed his forehead to hers. "Sorry for scaring you. I just found out Faelin is my half brother."

Jasmine jerked back. "What?"

He told her what Sable told them at the meeting. "Faelin is old enough that dear ole dad created Faelin before he mated with Mom. Which means Royce had always been a rogue bastard."

That was before Jasmine's time, so she couldn't confirm or deny that Royce was anything but a rogue. The male was always a bastard as she remembered him. "I'm sorry."

Dane stood and held out his hand. "Want to go for a run? Let our wolves out to play?"

Every part of her lit up with desire at his words. Her wolf was so ready to play with his. She took his hand and allowed him to pull her to a stand. Instead of stepping back, he stayed where he was so their bodies pressed together when she stood. Then he wrapped his arms around her and held her close while nuzzling her neck.

He trembled slightly and she sank into his embrace. He was her mate. There was no denying the pulling. "Are you sure you are ready to mate with all my chaos?"

A chuckle vibrated from him. "Chaos one and two will eventually mature. The training program will help them."

He lifted his head and scanned her face before his gaze landed on her lips. Desire heated her insides. She didn't wait for him to kiss her. She rose on her toes and captured his lips in a raw, unforgiving kiss. A feral growl escaped him as he lifted her and sat her on top of her desk.

"I need you, Jas." There was a vulnerability in his voice she'd never heard before.

"You have me. I'm not ready to complete the bond." She was afraid of the pain they went with feeling her mate die and part of her soul being ripped from her. She saw it the moment her dad died. Her mom dropped to the floor, screaming in pain and anguish of losing her mate.

He lifted her chin so she looked into his eyes. After a few moments, he smiled. "Let's go for that run."

They stripped down, then shifted into their wolves right before they exited out the back door of the bar.

Jasmine ran toward the tree line of the forest.

Dane gave chase. The pounding of his paws against the snow-covered ground, closing in on her, excited her. She squealed as anticipation of being caught by her wolf filled her.

The cold winter air blew through her white fur and it felt amazing. She loved winter, especially when the snow blanketed the earth.

When she reached the first layer of the wards that protected Ashwood from the outside world, she stopped and glanced at Dane over her shoulder. He yipped at her and didn't slow down. That told her she was good to go outside the wards.

Trusting her mate, she rushed forward, knowing right where she wanted to go. There was a waterfall and a river not far from the den. Even though the water would be freezing, she still loved to splash around in it.

She reached the waterfall, Dane caught her. He tackled her to the ground and penned her to the ground. She nuzzled his neck, then bit playfully. Jumping off her, he bounced around on his paws before he took off through the forest, wanting her to chase him.

Laughing, she ran after him. When was the last time she just let her wolf out to play? Her and the twins used to go for runs all the time. Then her fear of losing them—her only family she had left—to the mutants made her confine them to the den.

She slowed and her heart ached. She was restricting them from being kids.

Dane barked at her, drawing her attention. Then he growled. A laugh bubbled up inside her. Her mate didn't like her mood change. He'd have to deal with it. She was a female and moody.

But he was right, now wasn't the time to think about all the things she'd failed at in being the twins' guardian. She'd fix it. They could be a happy family again. She would make sure of it.

About an hour later, Jasmine and Dane stood under the hot sprays of her shower. She was still shivering from being out in the snow. Dane circled her with his arms and held her under the water.

"I can't remember the last time I ran like that." She pressed her cold nose against his chest, which made him jerk and grunt at her.

"Me neither. We should take the boys out next time. But don't stay out in the snow as long." Dane kissed her forehead and rubbed her arms. "Are you warming up?"

"Yeah." She peered into his gaze and gave him a wicked smile. "I know what would heat me up more."

"Really? And what would that be?" His lips lifted in a sensual grin that made her pussy ache.

"Really." She gripped his cock and slowing stroked it. A growl-like groan escaped him and he rolled his hips forward, pressing his hard length into her.

His wolf flashed in his eyes and he turned her around so her back was flat against his front. Lifting one of her legs, he entered her with a quick thrust. The sudden invasion stung but she relished in the feel of him filling her.

"Fuck. You feel amazing milking my cock." He slid a hand down her stomach to finger her clit. Her body jerked as pleasure rolled through her in fiery waves.

Dane rolled his hips, increasing his thrusts. Each forward motion pushed him deeper and deeper, hitting the right spot to send her over the edge. But she held on, not wanting it to end.

She bent forward, giving him better access. Damn, it felt good. Dane felt amazing as he commanded her body to obey him. She wasn't naturally a submissive wolf, but for him, she'd be anything he wanted as long as he pleasured her.

"I'm going to mark you, let every-fucking-body know who you belong to."

Fuck, yes. She straightened and turned her head to give him full access to her neck. That was all the permission he needed. He struck, sinking his wolf fangs into her skin. She cried out as pain melted away into pleasure so intense, her orgasm exploded within her.

He slammed into her over and over. Their breaths came in short gasps and pants. Another orgasm was building and she knew she would be able to hold onto that one. Then his body tensed behind her and he tightened his hold her as his hot seed spilled inside her.

After a few seconds, Dane pulled out and grabbed the soap and washed her. She sighed, loving the way he was taking care of her. One of the many perks to having a mate.

She frowned as she pushed away tears before they formed, but there was no hiding her whirl of emotions from Dane. As an empath, he was too in tune with her and his family.

After they washed and rinsed the soap off, they

got out of the shower. Jasmine wrapped herself in a large bath towel. When she reached her bed, Dane asked, "What's wrong?"

"When my dad died, I was with Mom. She tried to dull her pain from me, but I still felt it." Jasmine closed her eyes. Her nose tingled as the tears formed. "Then the pain of losing her. It doesn't go away. You never forget it."

Dane closed the distance. He took her towel off and dried her skin, then motioned to the bed. She sat and he went to her dresser. "What are you doing?"

"Getting you dressed."

She laughed. "You don't need to take care of me."

"Yes I do." He pulled out a pair of black lace thongs and tossed them to her. Then the matching bra followed. "You do so much for those boys and the bar and your employees. When do you have time for you?"

"I have about an hour of quiet time before I go to sleep at night. Sometimes I'll wake up early and enjoy some alone time before the boys get up."

He dug out a pair of jeans and a t-shirt and moved back to her. "Quiet time is good. But when was the last time you went off and did something completely selfish for yourself. Treat yourself to... whatever females do?"

Frowning she thought about it. She was in her teens when she last treated herself to anything. When she turned eighteen, she worked in the bar and learned everything she could about running it. Plus she loved the time she spent with her mom by working beside her every day.

Dane lifted her chin. "Mom didn't have time or the ability to block Hayden, Tanner, and me from the impact of killing Royce. We all felt it. Her pain as their souls ripped apart when she drove the knife into his heart. The rage Mom felt as she did it."

Jasmine gasped. She knew Luna had killed her mate to protect the Pack and her boys, but never knew the details of it. Glancing at Dane's fisted hands, Jasmine wrapped hers around his and brought them to her lips. "Does it scare you that we'll end up feeling that pain?"

He sank to his knees so they were eye to eye. "Every fucking day. But I'd rather have a bond with you and feel you alive inside me so I know you are safe than to lose you before that happens."

Damn. He sure makes it hard to deny him. Why was she?

Before she could say anything, he kissed her softly. "Get dressed, I'll cook dinner then we'll watch a movie with the boys."

He stood and slid his jeans on then left her room. He had stolen her heart a long time ago. It was time she admitted it to herself and be an adult about it. And claim her mate.

CHAPTER EIGHT

Luna sank into her oversized beanbag, a book in one hand and a glass of wine in the other. The house was so quiet and had been since her boys moved out. Tanner still lived with her, but he wasn't home much. He usually hung out with Kirk or was patrolling the perimeter of Ashwood territory with a couple of other sentries. Lately, he'd been working with Jonathan, the newest member of the Pack.

She sensed something more than a friendship starting between the males, but she didn't ask questions. The relationship would blossom on its own time.

Dane was with Jasmine, which made Luna

happy. Jasmine was a good mate for her son. Just like Christa was for Hayden.

Even though she was happy for her sons, she had a longing to share her life with someone. After Royce, she swore she'd never love again. She made those promises in a fit of rage and pain.

In truth, she wanted a mate. It was time for her to start looking for one. Yet, none of the males in the den sparked her wolf's interest. Or maybe she just wasn't ready.

A knock sounded on her back door. Frowning she called to her wolf to surface and went to the door. She flipped in the porch light and opened, ready to give whoever it was a taste of her Alpha power.

When she saw him, her heart dropped to her feet and she gasped and backed up. No. It couldn't be. If she hadn't been the one to kill Royce herself, she'd sworn the rogue bastard rose from the dead.

Rafe Raines. Her brother-in-law and Royce's twin brother stood at her back door.

She folded her arms and didn't move to let him in. "What do you want?"

"Hello, to you too, Luna." He lifted a brow, then racked his gaze over her, making her body heat up.

What the fuck? No way was Rafe her mate. Not fucking happening!

"Why are you here?" She'd ask how he got in, but she knew the answer. The same way Faelin did. His intent wasn't to harm anyone. It still didn't make him wanted.

"I've come to warn you."

She laughed although there was no humor behind it. "You're too late. Good bye."

She went to slam the door, but he stuck his foot in the jam, block it. "I know you don't want to see me. Hell, I can't even look at myself in the mirror without seeing that bastard."

Damn. She didn't want to feel sorry for him. "You left. I thought I could count on you to have my back."

He reached for her and she jumped back. Touching Rafe would be a mistake. The movement gave him room to step inside her house. She shook her head. "You need to go."

"I left because Royce said he'd kill you and the boys if I stayed."

She froze. "He what? Why would he say that? Besides he was crazy."

Rafe locked gazes with her. One of the differences in him and Royce were their eyes. Royce had navy blue eyes while Rafe's were ice blue. Rafe's hair was pitch black. "Because he knew I loved you."

What? She whirled around, giving him her back. He what? *Okay, Luna, breath.* This wasn't happening. Every night for the last week, she'd had a reoccurring vision where a male would say those exact words. It told her she'd meet another mate soon, but she wasn't sure who or when.

"Lu." He stepped closer and she closed her eyes. Rafe and Keegan were the only ones to call her Lu. Keegan did it because they were long time friends. Even before they merged the Packs. "I came to warn you about Faelin."

"He's Royce's son. I know." She moved to her beanbag and picked up her wine and drained the contents.

Rafe followed her to the kitchen. "How do you know?"

"Sable Darwin is mated to our Pack Justice." Luna turned to watch he reaction.

He wasn't surprised by that little bit of news. "I know. Before you ask, I've been watching over you and the den. The move to merge with Ashwood was smart. It made sense because you and Keegan were friends."

Leaning against the counter, she studied him. He looked like he aged since the last time she saw him. Shifters didn't start to show signs of aging until they were well over a thousand. Hard living and stress can cause them to age as well.

"Where have you been?" She moved to the fridge and pulled out a bottle of beer and handed it to him.

He took it. "Thanks." After opening it and taking a drink, he answered her question. "After I left, I went in search of the rebel groups. I knew they were out there and not all of them were against shifters."

Jared had said he found Rafe in a rebel group, but Luna wasn't sure she wanted to go search him out. She still wasn't sure she wanted him in her house. He brought too many emotions to the forefront. Too much pain, she wasn't ready to deal with.

"Jared said you were working with the rebels."

Rafe sat at the kitchen nook and start picking at the label of his long neck. "We mostly kept the human rebel groups from discovering the truth about shifters and gave them false leads away from dens. I found out about Faelin about a year ago. Rumors were circulating through the groups that Felix had a son just as crazy as he was and that was a mutant that could shift."

"Too crazy to not look into." Luna frowned and sat across from him.

"Yeah. And be careful what you go searching for." Rafe shook his head. "I knew when I saw him that he was not Felix's son. Have you seen Faelin up close? Looked into his blood crazed eyes?"

Luna shook her head. "Faelin had shown up a month ago and kidnapped a group of kids to use in his mutant army. No one except Sable, Ana, and Jared had been close enough to the male. Then the bastard materializes inside the wards to confront Sable a few days ago. That was when she recognized who he really was."

"He's crazy. It goes beyond bloodlust and going rogue." Rafe finished off his beer before continuing. "I have a few men on the inside at Onyx. Right now it's not clear what Faelin wants except for revenge for Felix's death. But if he knows the male was not his father, then there is no telling what his plan is now. I got a report this morning that Faelin is looking for a pendent. It's a wolf carved from moonstone. I'm not sure why he'd be looking for it."

That sounded odd. "Moonstones can harvest the power of the moon and can strengthen psychic abilities. But mostly it's used for healing and protection."

Rafe nodded. "I recalled that Royce had one. I

found it in his desk and asked if it was for you. Royce went crazy and we fought. That was when he told me to leave."

Luna frowned. She'd never seen the pendant. Knowing what she did and thinking back, she wondered if it belonged to Faelin's mother. Or someone else. But since Faelin was looking for it, she was betting it was his mother. "Do you think it's still with his things in MoonRiver?"

She left all of Royce's belongings in the rubble of what was left of her old den. She had considered burning the place down. It was a good thing that she didn't.

"There's only one way to find out."

Luna met his gaze. They'd have to go search the ruins of MoonRiver. "We'll assemble a team to go look. No one goes off alone anymore. My sons will insist on being there. And seeing you will not be easy on them. So I need to give them a heads up."

"Yeah." He frowned.

"And Tanner lives here, so be prepared to face him in the morning, if he comes home tonight." Luna stood. "You can take one of the spare rooms up stairs. Tanner's room is the last one on the left. I'm going to bed."

She left Rafe sitting at the table and shut herself

inside her bedroom. What the fuck was she going to tell her sons?

CHAPTER NINE

It was the first day Jasmine had taken off since her parents died. And it felt great. She slept in and was still in her PJs at 4:00 in the afternoon. She had gone out onto the balcony that overlooked the bar from her upstairs apartment to check on things.

Dane and her were up late the night before talking about everything and anything—their childhoods, his brothers and all the trouble they used to get into. Her feelings for Dane were growing. The more she was with him, the more she wanted to wake up with him every morning.

Like that morning. He had coffee made and was cooking breakfast by the time she got out of the shower. She was starting to see that being with him would outweigh her fear of losing him.

Life was about risks.

Jasmine exited her bedroom and crossed the living room just as the door to her apartment opened and Cole stormed in. He locked gazes with her and threw his backpack toward her. It missed her by a few inches and slammed against the wall behind her.

"What the hell is wrong with you?" Anger rose up inside her and it took all her control to not beat his ass. His anger was getting out of hand.

"You screw everything up!"

What did she do now? "How am I screwing up your life now?"

"I couldn't train today." He glared at her, his wolf in his eyes.

Yeah, she knew. But he caused it on himself.

"And how is that my fault? Dane and I told you that you had to stay out of trouble and keep your grades up. Then I get a call from Rhea this morning saying you were suspended for two days. Care to explain to me why?" Jasmine crossed her arms, letting her own wolf peak out of her eyes.

He threw his hands up in the air and stalked to her. She braced herself. He may only be nine, but his wolf was strong and he was starting to bulk up. Kids from the age of eight to sixteen go through so many changes. They grew the fastest during those years, slowing down when they reached about sixteen, then stopping altogether when they reach eighteen.

Cole snarled. "You know why. It was a stupid joke. It's not my fault no one in that school has a sense of humor. And it happened last week, before we made our deal."

Was he serious? "It doesn't matter. You should have disclosed this joke when we talked about it yesterday. Lay out all your little dark secrets before they bite you in the ass. You will not train for a week. And don't go to Dane about this because he has my back on it."

"That's not fair! I hate you!" He stormed off to his room and slammed the door.

Jasmine closed her eyes and took deep breaths. May the gods, keep her calm.

When she opened her eyes, she noticed Luna standing in the doorway. Jasmine offered her a weak smile before it turned into a frown. How long had she been there? "Hi, Momma Wolf."

She came in and shut the door behind her. Then she crossed the room to her, drawing her into a hug. "He's not angry at you."

"Yeah I keep telling myself that too." Jasmine

hugged Luna back, loving the feel of a motherly embrace.

Pulling back, Jasmine studied her. Luna looked...lost. Which was weird because she was the strongest person Jasmine knew. "Are you okay?"

She shrugged and sat on the sofa. Pulling one of the square pillows into her lap, Luna stared at the backpack Cole threw. "Boys bottle up their emotions. The training will help him, once he's off restriction."

Jasmine sighed joined Luna on the couch. "Yeah, I think so too. I wasn't sure at first. But Dane can be pretty persuasive."

"That's my son." Luna fell quiet again and Jasmine knew something was bothering her. Before she could ask her again what as wrong, Luna said, "Rafe is back."

Jasmine stared at Luna with her mouth open. "As in your brother-in-law?"

"The one and only." Luna frowned. "I'm not sure how I feel about it."

Why was Luna talking to her about that? Then it dawned on her. Luna didn't have many female friends. She worked 24/7, protecting the Pack and being an Alpha. Sometimes it was easy to forget that she could fall apart like the rest of them.

Luna and Jasmine's mom were best friends.

Jasmine had grown up around Luna. Even though she tried not to notice, Jasmine saw what Royce put Luna through. That was another reason Jasmine hesitated when it came to mating Dane. But Dane was nothing like his psycho father.

"Why is he back? Is he staying?"

Luna met her gaze. "He says he came to warn me about Faelin. But we already knew that. Did Dane tell you?"

"That he has a new half brother? Yeah." Jasmine watched her Alpha.

"I'm sorry to unload on you. I didn't know where else to go." Luna started to get up but Jasmine grabbed her hands, stopping her.

"I feel honored and blessed that you came to me. After all you and Mom were best friends and I'll be your daughter-in-law soon." Jasmine smiled at her.

Luna's features softened. "So you are finally giving in?"

Jasmine laughed. "I think Dane has suffered enough. Although I'm not sure he knows what he's getting himself into. Those boys, especially Cole, are a handful."

"It's Karma. Hayden and Dane were hellions."

"Yeah, he told me about all the trouble they got into." She glanced at Cole's backpack, still not believing he threw it at her. But she knew he missed on purpose. Shaking her head, she met Luna's stare. "Some of the females are going out to the old cabin Dani lived in before meeting Nevan for an all-girl slumber party. Come with me."

Lunas features brightened. "Are you sure?"

"Hell yeah. It'll be fun. We'll drink, eat, and talk about boys." Jasmine grinned, hoping that Luna would say yes. She never did anything with the females and this would allow her to connect with them more. "Unless you want to sit at home with Rafe."

Luna crinkled her nose. "Count me in."

"Great!" Jasmine jumped up. "I'll grab my bag and then we'll go to your place and get your things."

Jasmine rushed to her room. She'd packed her overnight bag earlier that afternoon since she took the day off and needed something to do. The apartment was spotless. When she passed by Cole's room, she knocked on it. "I'm heading out. I'll be at the Pack cabin. Dane will be here soon to stay with you."

The door opened. He wasn't as angry as he was when he came in. "I don't need a babysitter."

"Tough. Dane is staying anyway." When she turned to walk away, he touched her arm.

"I'm sorry."

"I'll be scheduling some time for you to talk to Nevan. I'm not going to be the object of your anger. Nor will I tolerate you yelling at me and throwing things at me. You're growing up and it's time you deal with everything." Jasmine was done. She loved her brothers and wanted to protect them and keep them safe. But she couldn't do that if they didn't help themselves.

"What about Kyle?"

"He's already talking with Nevan."

Cole jerked back in surprise. "He didn't tell me."

Jasmine sighed. "He doesn't have to tell you everything."

"I guess." Cole glanced down the hallway toward the living room. "I'll go apologize to Luna."

"Thank you." Jasmine pulled him into a hug. "I miss them too. Every damn day. I'm not perfect but I try to be. You don't make it easy for me."

"I'm trying." He kept his tone soft and she heard the crack in his voice. "I'll meet with Nevan."

Pulling back she framed his face. "Training will help too, after you are done with restriction. Or maybe you can offer to do community service around the den. Talk to Dane about it tonight. But I mean it. No more trouble. Pranks and jokes are fun, but you push it into another level."

He smiled then. "I'll talk to Dane. I really want to be an Enforcer like Dad was."

"He would be so proud." She kissed his forehead and motioned to the living room. "Go talk to Luna."

He nodded and rushed down the hall. Jasmine shook her head. She wouldn't relive her adolescent years for all the money in the world. It's a confusing and emotional time.

She took her time grabbing her bag to give him and Luna a few minutes to talk. While she waited, she texted Dane.

Heading to the cabin. Your mom is going.

Dane: That will be great for her. Thanks for including her.

Jasmine: No problem. I love Momma Wolf.

He typed something then stopped. Then started typing again.

Dane: Have fun. There will be sentries in the area.

She smiled. That was Dane talk for he cared. Her heart fluttered and her fingers hovered over the keys. She typed, "Love you," then stared at the words. When the hell had that happened? The words were effortless and without a thought of what she'd say.

However, she wasn't sure it was the right time to tell him that so she deleted it and instead typed, **See you tomorrow night**.

Smoke rolled out of the chimney of the cabin when Jasmine and Luna arrived. Good someone was there already. Jasmine was usually early for everything and she hoped she wouldn't be the first one to arrive at the cabin.

"Looks like we're not first." Jasmine smiled wide at Luna. "Is it bad that I'm way too happy to be away from the boys?"

Laughing Luna shook her head. "No, that's part of being a mom. You love them and will do anything for them, but when you are away from them, you're free."

The door flew open and Shay's smiling face greeted them. She looked at Luna and squealed. "Momma's here!" She pulled Luna into a hug. "You come to join in on our mischief?"

"Yep. It's been a while since I stirred up trouble."

Luna entered the cabin and Jasmine followed, giving Shay a hug after she closed the door.

"It's supposed to snow again tonight." Shay disappeared into the kitchen. When she came back, she had a large bowl of chips and some small bowls with dips and salsa in them. "I'm glad I came early to get the fire started. I turned the heat on upstairs."

Shay was a white tiger. Cats typically got colder than wolves did, even neither of the species felt the cold like humans did. But a fire and warmth was always a good thing in the middle of January in the mountains.

"What's on the agenda for tonight?" Jasmine took off her jacket and hung it on the coat rack near the door.

"Well, the only way to get Cam to come was to promise to set up the nanny cam." Shay laughed. "That will be entertaining to watch Graham and Blaine take care of the triplets."

"For sure," Luna said just as her phone rang. Frowning she pulled it out of her back pocket and stared at it. "What?" She paused and met Jasmine's gaze then rolled her eyes. "Girls night. I'll be back tomorrow... that's not up to you." She worked her jaw and her wolf entered her eyes. "Look, we'll talk about it tomorrow…My sons know where I'm at…I'm hanging up now."

She hung up and and Shay glanced from Luna to Jasmine. "Should I ask?"

Luna typed on her phone as she answered. "Rafe is back." When she was done with her text, she added, "He's my problem and I'll deal with him when I'm ready."

She turned off her phone and tossed it on the kitchen counter.

"Rafe…" Shay stared at Luna for a while then nodded. "The MIA brother-in-law. Sorry."

Luna shrugged. "He's not a threat to the Pack or he wouldn't be in my house. Tanner will deal with him."

The cabin door opened drawing their attention to Cameron, Dani, and Sasha as they entered. Cameron's features lit up when she noticed Luna. "Now you know it's going to be one hell of a party when Luna shows."

"You girls don't have to pretend to want me here." She winked and pulled each of the females into hugs. "I feel like we should do something wicked."

"What do you have in mind?" Cameron asked with a little too much enthusiasm.

CHAPTER TEN

It was mid-morning and Dane hadn't heard from his mom or his mate. He was getting worried.

"You okay?" Christa asked as she entered the Pack circle.

"Yeah. Jasmine's not home yet."

Christa shrugged. "They most likely stay up all night and are still sleeping."

She was right. Dane was worrying for nothing. "I asked you to come because I want to make sure I'm not calling a pissed-off spirit."

Christa drew her brows together. "Honestly I'm not sure. When Rick died he was a mutant and was with Gina when Hayden and I found her. Gina had given him the same counter agent she took, but he didn't react well to it."

"Do you know why he would show himself to Bryce?"

Christa shook her head and turned as her niece and nephew walked into the circle. "You ready? He may not be the same person he was."

"We know," Brenna said as she gripped her brother's hand.

"We feel that he needs to tell us something." Bryce glanced at Brenna then to Dane. "We're ready."

Dane moved to the center of the circle, which was lined with rocks from the nearby river. Each stone had a rune craved in it for blessings, protection, and health. Dane took the salt he brought with him and outlined a circle that would contain the ghost when he called to it.

When the salt circle was complete he set the container on the ground and held his hands out to his sides. He closed his eyes and stretched his senses out to the surrounding area of the circle and further, searching for a ghost with a similar signature as the twins. Since Rick was a wolf, as the teens were, it wouldn't be hard to match his imprint. Although

Dane wasn't sure if that was still the case since Rick died as a mutant.

He found Christa's aura, then Brenna's and Bryce's. Just behind Bryce was his father. "Rick, I call you to my circle."

Moments later the ghost appeared. He was transparent at first then took on a corporeal form. He had black hair like the twins and looked mostly human with a few mutant features. Glancing at Dane, Rick stepped forward but stopped at the edge of the salt. "Why am I contained?"

"I wasn't sure what your state of mine was in. I'm protecting the twins as well as my Pack." Dane let his power surface, showing Rick that he could make him vanish as easily as he made him appear.

Rick glanced away and stared at Christa. Sadness flowed from him as he looked at his sister-in-law. "I didn't kill Mary. She was my mate, my everything until the twins came and completed our family." He glanced to Brenna and Bryce. "You have to believe me."

"Then what happen the day Mary died?" Christa asked with steel in her tone.

"I was working undercover in the Onyx Pack. Ashwood Falls wasn't the only Pack trying to bring down the rogue. Ashwood just had more balls to go in and do something about the problem." Rick began pacing his circle. "Felix discovered that I was a spy and injected me with the serum. During my transformation, he ordered Mary and the twins to be killed."

Sorrow rolled from the twins and Dane stepped back so they could lean on him and connect with his wolf. As the Beta, one of his jobs was to be the support of the Pack. Sometimes the youth needed to connect with an adult wolf for additional strength. Adults did too, but not as much. Especially with all the shit MoonRiver and Ashwood had been through.

"Why are you here?" Bryce asked.

Rick watched them. "Faelin. He's insane but a genius. He was always searching for a way to gain power. He has no natural magick. Everything he can do is because of a demon."

"A demon?"

Rick nodded. "He has one held prisoner somewhere. It was in Onyx but he moved it when you took back the kids he stole. He moved all the mutants."

"Are you sure it's a demon?"

Rick met Dane's stare. "I felt its dark magick when I searched the den a few days ago."

A demon held against its will was never a good thing. It could break free and then no one would be safe from its wrath. "How is he using the demon's power?"

"By drinking its blood," Brenna said. Her tone was flat. "Is he going to bond with it?"

Her last question carried notes of fear. Bryce shook his head. "If he bonds with the demon, it will be worse than Felix and Savannah. And I'm not sure Ana and Sable are strong enough to stop them."

Rick moved closer to Dane again. "I want to help. I can search for the demon and spy for you."

Dane ran a hand through his hair. He couldn't stop the ghost from being there. By the sounds of it he's been around for a while. Probably since the day he died. And he didn't pick up any aggression from Rick.

With the toe of his shoe, he brushed away the salt, breaking the circle. Rick stumbled out and rushed to the twins. Christa stiffened as Rick gathered his kids into a tight hug.

Dane stepped back to give the kids some space with their father. Christa moved back with him. "How long will he stay solid?"

"It's hard to say. I can't control that part of my power. Usually a few minutes. The longest I had a ghost in a corporeal state was an hour." Dane looked at his phone. "Where are the females?"

Jared crossed the field to them. He looked pissed. Well, more so than normal. Dane faced him and lifted a brow. "What's wrong with you?"

"My mate is not hanging out with your mother anymore."

"What has our fearless Alpha done now?"

Jared growled. "Apparently, it was Luna's idea to go bar hopping in Boone. All eight females were arrested this morning. As their lawyer, I have to go bail them out."

What the fuck? "Arrested? For what?"

"I don't know. I assume there was a large amount of alcohol involved. However, two of the females are pregnant and don't drink. Not sure what their excuse is." Jared started walking back toward the center of the den.

Christa was laughing but she managed to say, "Go ahead. I'll take care of Rick and update everyone later."

Dane jogged after Jared. "We can take the van then play the music loud on the way home."

"If the Healers haven't healed their hangovers yet." Jared cut left to head to the school and nursery to get one of the vans.

They made the drive to Boone in under forty-five minutes. Going the speed limit, it would have taken an hour, but Jared apparently was in a hurry.

Dane followed Jared inside the police station. So the females didn't actually go to jail, they were being held until they sobered up. His mom as never going to live it down. And neither was his mate, now that he thought about it.

They went to the receptionist's desk and Jared told the officer they were there to pick the females.

Several minutes passed before the females filed out from the holding area. Sable was in front and she looked like she was holding in a laugh. Leave it up to Sable to find getting arrested fun. She walked up to Jared and pressed a kiss to his lips. He growled at her, which made her laugh harder.

Luna met Dane's glare and she shook her head. "Don't ask. But I'm sure Dani and Sable will tell you all about it."

Jasmine walked with Rhea and Cameron, followed by Shay, Dani, and Sasha. If it wasn't for the smell of alcohol, he wouldn't guess they'd been out causing trouble. Dane growled low. "Please tell me none of you shifted in front of humans."

Luna frowned. "I don't think so." She looked at Sable then Dani—the two pregnant females that didn't drink.

Dani shook her head. "Sable and I did good in keeping the animals on the inside. Clothing was optional."

She burst out laughing, which made Sable laugh.

"This was the best night ever. We have got to do it again," Sable said in between laughs.

Luna walked toward the doors. "Next time with less alcohol. Let's go home. I have to deal with the twin of my dead mate."

"What?" Dane moved passed her and blocked the door. "Rafe is here?"

Luna pressed a hand to her forehead. "Not here. In the den. My house."

Jasmine walked up to him and wrapped her arms around his waist and rested her head against his chest. "I need sleep and a bottle of aspirin. Dani won't heal our headaches. She was being mean."

"Good," Dane rumbled and kissed her forehead. "Let's go home."

CHAPTER ELEVEN

Dane took Jasmine home while his mom and the other females went to their homes to sleep off their hangovers. After he tucked Jasmine into her bed, he went to his mom's house.

He knocked on the door and Rafe answered. A mix of anger and happy-to-see-him swirled inside him. The anger came from seeing his father's face. Yet, Dane was happy to see his uncle after years of him being MIA. Then anger returned for not hearing from him. "Rafe."

"Dane."

Pushing past him, Dane entered his mom's home. "Why are you here?"

Rafe shut the door and followed him into the living room. "I came to warn Luna of Faelin."

Dane glared at him. "And what do you know of him?"

"That he's Royce's son and he's insane."

Dane snorted. He couldn't help it. "You're a few days late with that info. Did you know he is holding a demon hostage and drawing from its power?"

He frowned. But it was Dane's mom who spoke as she entered the living room, her hair wet from a shower. "What demon?"

Rafe added, "I didn't know of a demon. How do you?"

"A ghost told me." Dane locked gazes with his mom. "Bryce saw Rick the other day and Hayden sent him my way. So before Jared and I came to pick you and the other females up, I was in the pack circle with the Baker twins calling the ghost of their dead father."

He told them everything Rick had said. "So the raid to get the children from his underground lab forced him to move his mutants and the demon."

Luna turned to Rafe. "I thought you said you had spies in Onyx."

"I do but they haven't gotten close enough to Faelin, yet. The bastard doesn't trust anyone. Not even his own Beta, Easton." Rafe pulled out his phone and sent a text. "I'll find out where he might have taken the demon, but it'll take some time. Meanwhile, we need to go searching for the moonstone pendant."

Dane glanced at the two in confusion. "What pendant?"

Luna rubbed her head and moved to the kitchen while talking to them. "It's a wolf craved from moonstone. Rafe saw Royce with one and we think it might be with his stuff at MoonRiver."

"When were you going to search?"

Luna came back into the living room with a bottle of water. "Tomorrow. I need to let Blaine and the Elders know what's up. Today, I'm sleeping."

And Dane had a date with his mate, whether she knew it or not.

JASMINE GAVE up on trying to sleep. As soon as she entered the apartment the boys smelled the alcohol on her and started with the jokes. So there she was, stretched out on the sofa with an icepack and a large bottle of water.

A knock sounded on the door and she groaned. She was in no mood for visitors. Cole jumped up and answered it. "Hi, Dane! Jasmine got drunk last night."

She threw a pillow at Cole. It hit him in the back and he laughed. "Don't start a pillow fight Jas."

She growled. "Please don't. Go get me something for my head."

Dane appeared in her line of sight and shook his head. She sat up and he settled beside her. "Rafe is back."

"I know. Luna told me." Jasmine leaned her head on his shoulder. Her head was starting to ease. "Kyle, can you make me a sandwich?"

"Yep." He disappeared into the kitchen.

"I'm glad our natural shifter healing abilities help with hangovers. I couldn't imagine how humans deal with feeling this way."

"Well, humans can't drink as much as we can." Dane chuckle and she pinched his side.

"It's not funny. I didn't have nearly as much as Luna and Cameron." Jasmine chuckled and then wished she didn't.

Cole came back with some meds. She took them. "Thanks."

"You're welcome." Her brother smirked and went back to flipping through the TV channels.

Kyle came back with a huge tray of food. She

arched her brow at him and he shrugged. "I made enough for everyone."

"That was thoughtful." She picked a sandwich and bit into it. After she chewed it, she said, "After lunch, do you guys want to go for a run? Well, you guys can run, I'll just tag along behind you."

Dane chuckled again. "Actually shifting into your wolf should help with the hangover."

That was what she was thinking too. Plus it'd be good for the boys to let their wolves out.

Cole asked, "Why don't we pack everything up and have a picnic?"

"We can." She studied Cole for a long moment and realized he liked having Dane around. Even when Dane was getting on to him for the stupid shit he did, Cole was respectful to him. Unlike how he mouthed off to Jasmine.

The boys rushed into motion. Kyle turned off the TV and helped Cole pack everything up. Jasmine frowned. "I'm a bad mom-sister. I haven't taken them out for a run in so long."

"There's been a lot going on. The scare with the kidnapping didn't help any of us feel secure." Dane stood and offered his hand.

She took it and pulled herself up. "Yeah. That and I work too much."

The boys came back into the living room with a basket and a blanket. "We're ready!"

"Okay then. Let's go." Jasmine opened the apartment door and crinkled her nose. The smells of the bar below churned her stomach. "I'll never drink that much again."

Dane laughed and nudged her to go. "You might."

He was right, but she wasn't going to tell him that. She descended the stairs and made it out the door before anyone saw her. If her employees asked her something, she'd get roped into working.

Not today. She was relaxing and spending much needed time with her brothers and her mate.

She let the boys choose where they wanted to run. Surprisingly, it wasn't too far from the bar, but it was outside the first layer of wards. Which from what Luna said the night before, Faelin could get in.

The sound of a low growl, more like a yowl caught her attention and she looked up. A leopard laid lazily on a thick branch. Alec.

Seeing him there made Jasmine relax a little more. The boys noticed him too. They set the basket and blanket on the ground and shifted into their wolves. Then they circled the tree. "Boys, leave Alec alone."

The boys ran off into the woods. Jasmine could

hear them so she didn't worry, too much. Dane wrapped his arms around her and yanked her to him, then he kissed her. Raw passion exploded inside her, and she pressed into him. Too soon he broke the kiss. "What did you females do to get arrested?"

Jasmine rolled her eyes. "I think the cops were just checking on us. I'm not really sure what drew their attention. Everything is a little fuzzy. Then Luna started making demands saying she was the Alpha and no male was going to order her around."

"Mom doesn't get out much." He chuckled.

"It's why I invited her to come. And in my defense, who am I to deny the Alpha a good time." She batted her lashes.

Dane picked the blanket up and spread it out. "You're guilty by association."

"Ha. I'm still sticking to my story. I was following Alpha orders."

He studied her for a few moments. "The reason Luna will get away with this is because there were two Enforcers and the Hunter with y'all. Otherwise, Hayden would give her hell for it. The Alphas aren't to be outside the den without Enforcers." He paused as if thinking about it. "But both Healers were with you."

Yeah there was that. "I know. The original plan

was to stay at the cabin, drink, and talk shit about the males."

Suddenly the forest fell silent. Jasmine turned in a circle, searching for the boys. "What's going on?" Then she smelled them. "Mutants."

She went to yell for the boys until Dane motioned for her to stay quiet. Fear gripped her gut. Taking a deep breath, she recalled what her father taught her about fighting rogues and mutants.

A wolf sounded several yards into the thick of the forest. It was followed by another almost identical. The boys! She rushed forward and stopped as Faelin materialized in front of her.

Backing up, she kept her eyes on him. He moved with her until he lunged forward and grabbed her by the throat. She tried to scream, but no sound came out.

Dane faced her and snarled. "Faelin, let her go."

"She's my insurance."

Jasmine frowned. What kind of insurance? She needed to stay calm and to do so, she focused on Dane.

Faelin yanked her back into him, not letting go of her throat. "I need your gift of life."

Dane pressed his lips in a thin line before answering. "I don't have the gift to give life."

"Lies. I saw you call a ghost and bring him to life."

Dane worked his jaw. "It doesn't work like that. If you want to talk to someone I can call to their spirit, but only if they are still in this realm. If they passed onto the next life, I can't connect to them."

Just then Alec jumped out of the tree and growled, baring his teeth. A few minutes later a black wolf stepped behind Dane. Jasmine recognized the wolf. It was Tanner. Relief flooded her.

"Faelin, you should train your mutants to be better fighters," Ana said as she advanced toward them from the groupings of trees. She wiped her blade on her black jeans before sheathing it. "Let her go."

Faelin laughed and squeezed her throat, cutting off her breathing. Jasmine widened her eyes as she stared at Dane. She clawed at Faelin's arm, trying to get him to let go. It was no use.

Howls cut through the air again and her heart sank. The boys were coming and they were calling for help. *Please don't hurt my boys.*

She saw Cole first. He was a blur of black and silver fur as he barreled into Faelin. Kyle came at them from the other side. The impacts threw Faelin off balance and he let go of Jasmine. She stumbled forward and saw Ana pull out a gun, so Jasmine dropped to the ground.

Ana fired.

Jasmine looked at where Faelin was only to see nothing. He vanished.

Dane rushed to her and drew her into a hug. "Are you okay?"

She nodded and held onto him, inhaling his scent. "The boys?"

Dane chuckled as Cole and Kyle came up to her and leaned against her. "Two junior enforcers doing their job."

She pulled the two wolves into hugs. "You two scared me."

They yipped, then wiggled out of her arms and pranced around.

Ana said, "Sable, Robyn, and Travis will be strengthening the wards tonight. No one will be able to teleport into the den anymore. Alec and his tech team will be setting up an additional layer of security and cameras about two hundred yards out from the magickal wards."

Jasmine glanced around the area they were in. She didn't feel like going for a run anymore. The boys had theirs. "Let's go back home."

Faelin camouflaged himself with the surrounding trees and watched Dane with his mate and his packmates. His plan to take Dane's power as his own failed. All because the damn wolf says he couldn't bring the dead to life. But Faelin knew he could. Dane just hadn't tapped into his full powers.

There will be a day when Dane uses his powers and Faelin would be there to absorb them as his own. The power to raise the dead would strength his mutant army more than Felix ever could.

He teleported to his remote lab and stared down at his demon. The female had her hands and ankles bound for his safety. She was a feisty bitch. "Tell me where the moonstone is."

"Fuck you!"

He backhanded her then grabbed his silver blade. She watched it as he set it down on her arm, sticking the point into her skin. She screamed. The silver burned demons and witches. "If you want it to stop, you'll tell me where the moonstone is."

The pendent he was looking for contained a power his mother placed in there before she died. Faelin assumed Felix had taken it, but it was nowhere in the Onyx den.

"MoonRiver," Demon hissed out.

Faelin removed the blade and teleported from the demon's cell to his office at Onyx. If the moonstone was in MoonRiver, that meant Royce had it. Faelin was going to get what belonged to him.

CHAPTER TWELVE

Dane took Jasmine and the boys home. His wolf paced under the surface, wanting to get out and track down Faelin and finish him. End this war before it all starts. But there were too many unknowns. One of them being the demon he held captive. If Faelin died would the demon be set free to roam Earthside? If that happened, they had more shit to worry about than mutants.

"What are you thinking about?" Jasmine asked as she threaded her fingers through his hair.

"Just thinking about Faelin and wondering how he managed to trap and hold a demon." He glanced into her jade-color eyes.

She gave him a small smile and then kissed him lightly. "He would need to have something that belonged to the demon. Or could have summoned it into a trap of some kind. But the big question is, why does he have the demon in the first place?"

"Rick said Faelin's power comes from the demon. So he is drawing its power somehow. It's possible Faelin is seeking ways to grow that power. Why else would he come to me wanting me to use mine?" Dane frowned. He hadn't thought about it at the time, but Faelin could have found a way to absorb another's powers.

"He found a way to tap into others' powers and use them." Jasmine frowned. "What kind of emotions did you pick up from him?"

Dane shook his head. "Not much. Anger, confusion, envy. Nothing to tell me what he had planned."

She frowned and curled up beside him on the sofa. The boys had gone to bed a few minutes ago. "What's the plan?"

Jasmine never cared about getting involved with the Enforcers. She was strong enough and with the proper training would be kick ass. But she loved the bar and loved taking care of her brothers. Dane also knew she believed it was being an Enforcer that killed her father, because he died protecting Luna and the pack from mutants.

That was five years ago. Then a year later her

mother was attacked when she was out for a run. The sentries didn't get to her fast enough. Jasmine had stepped in as the twin's guardian. Ashwood Falls had increased security and was still strengthening the wards.

Now that they had a demon to worry about.

Dane took a breath and exhaled to clear his mind of all the tragedy they've all lived through. Then he answered Jasmine's questions about the plan. "Faelin is looking for a moonstone pendant. Mom, my brothers, Rafe, and I are going to MoonRiver tomorrow to search for it."

She sat up and locked gazes with him. "I want to come and help."

He hesitated and when he went to speak, she pressed a finger over his lips. "I wasn't asking."

One side of his mouth twitched as he studied her. He knew she could fight. Out in the forest earlier she was distracted and surprised. He guessed it was because she hadn't expected Faelin to teleport inside the wards. Neither was Dane, especially when his intent *was* to harm since he did grab Jasmine and tried to choke her.

Glancing at her neck, he caressed her smooth skin. Thank the gods for their rapid healing abilities.

Jasmine relaxed and leaned forward. "He caught

me off guard and I could hear the boys. It won't happen again."

Instead of replying to her, he captured her mouth in a hard, unforgiving kiss. She groaned and fisted her hand in his hair, then climbed onto his lap, straddling him. He hardened and slid his hand up her shirt, needing skin contact.

She opened, allowing him to slip his tongue into her mouth. Pleasure rolled through him and over his skin. Holding her to him, he stood. She wrapped her legs around his waist as he carried her to her bedroom.

He kicked the door closed as he entered the room. Breaking the kiss, he dropped her on her mattress. She laughed as she bounced, then reached for the waistband of his pants. Hunger swirled in her jade eyes, making them almost glow. He felt her wolf surface, brushing against his, who was just under his skin.

Fuck. His mate was hot.

With a smirk, she stood on her knees and walked across the bed to him. "You not changing my mind about not going with you tomorrow."

"Just distracting you."

"Hmm." She pulled on the hem of his shirt and he snatched it over his head, throwing it behind him.

She nipped at his chest, then took one of his nipples between her teeth. He jerked at sensation and gripped her hair and pulled. Staring up at him, she laughed.

"You're mine."

A wicked smile formed on her face and her wolf flashed in her eyes. "And my crazy life."

"I'll take all of the crazy." He released her hair pushed her back onto the mattress. Then he removed her jeans and panties. He lowered to his knees and lifted one of her legs so it draped over his shoulder. Pressing a kiss to her belly, he slid two fingers into her slick folds. A soft moan escaped her and she fisted his hair. A dull pain registered as she pulled on his hair and moved her hips, rubbing her clit against his fingers.

He leaned in and lapped at her bundle of nerves. Her grip on his hair tightened. Satisfaction ripped through him, knowing he was giving her pleasure. Too long. He'd wasted too much time. It was time to claim his mate.

He covered her pussy with his mouth and slid his fingers inside her. Her body tensed, then she began to move again, and met the tempo he set by fingering her. A couple of thrusts and a bite to her clit sent her over the edge. Her body jerked as the orgasm tore through her.

When he withdrew from her and rose to his feet, he met her drunken, desire-filled gaze. She hooked her legs around him and pulled him on top of her. In a flash, she rolled them over and straddled him.

She dipped her head and bit his lower lip as she guided him inside her. Pleasure surged through him, and he wrapped his arms around her and thrust deeper, no longer able to wait another moment. His wolf urged him to bite, to claim her. The man would lose the battle. The urge was too strong.

Jasmine cried out, scored her nails into his shoulders and rode him. Pleasurable pain fueled his desire to possess her inside and out. Increasing the tempo, he bit her in the tender spot where her throat met her shoulder. Her rich, sweet blood coated his tongue as his fangs broke the skin. By the way her body tensed at first he could tell she was shocked by the bite. He tightened his hold on her as their pleasure mingled and grew.

The iridescent threads of the mating bond formed and weaved together, forever linking them. Her emotions—a mix of happiness, sadness, and confusion—poured into his subconscious. A sense of wholeness surrounded him like he had found a piece of his soul he didn't know was missing.

Jasmine's pleasure crashed over him, intensifying his own. Her muscles tensed around his cock a moment before she screamed her release. He squeezed her hips and thrust twice more. His balls tightened as an orgasm pulled him over the edge.

CHAPTER THIRTEEN

*J*asmine walked beside Dane as they moved through the underground tunnels that connected Ashwood Falls den to MoonRiver. Luna and Keegan—the former leopard Alpha—had them built after the two Packs merged years ago. Luna and Rafe were a few yards ahead of them. Hayden and Tanner were behind them.

Footsteps up head made them freeze. They weren't expecting anyone else. Then Jasmine recognized Rhea's form. Beside her was her mate, Alec.

Rhea smiled and stopped when she reached Jasmine, then handed her a gun. "There are silver bullets in the cartridge. Mutants are sensitive to silver, but if you want to kill them, aim for the head."

Jasmine nodded, remembering her father telling her the same thing. Something about the serum that made them the mindless, half-human, half-animal creatures sensitive to silver and lead, but silver burned as it entered their bodies, providing the perfect distraction to finish them off.

Jasmine check the chamber and tested the weight on the 9mm before slipping it into the back waistband of her jeans. When she glanced at Dane, he was staring at her. "What?"

"Just admiring how hot my mate is."

She shoved his shoulder. "I'm just hope I don't have to use the weapon."

There was only a small chance of they wouldn't run into rogues or mutants because MoonRiver wasn't warded like Ashwood. The main reason was because they wanted the secondary den to look abandoned. Which was also a welcoming mat for lone wolves and other shifters who prefer to not live in a Pack. Travelers and nomads often stayed at abandoned buildings and places for a few days before moving on. Jasmine hoped they wouldn't run into any while there. Some could be as dangerous are rogues.

They exited the tunnel at the back of the den through an opening in the mountain it was tucked up against. Jasmine's heart sank at the state of the den. Even though it'd been a few months since they all had to stay at MoonRiver and fixed it up some, most of the buildings were still in ruins.

Memories of the day Felix attacked MoonRiver still haunted her. She was glad the boys hadn't lived through it.

Dane took her hand and led her to the center of the den, then they crossed over to the Alpha house. It was once a beautiful, large three-story mini-mansion. The top level of the house was gone. The north side, where Luna's bedroom was had been blown to hell. Royce hadn't slept in that room with her for months before the attack. As Jasmine remembered, the late Alpha hadn't been in the den at all.

"We should burn the place down when we find the pendant." Luna snarled as she entered the house through the large hole.

Jasmine glanced at Dane who work his jaw and tugged her to follow him in through the front door, which wasn't there any longer. "There are so many hiding places in the house that Royce could have hidden the pendent so search anywhere and everywhere."

Moving through the living room to the kitchen, she searched in every small and large space she could think of with no luck. She was sure Luna had searched the obvious places like the safe in the office.

It was about an hour later before Rafe called out to everyone, "Found it."

He was in Tanner's old room and standing in front of the dresser. Luna moved forward. "Where was it?"

Rafe pointed at the mirror, then pressed the top right corner. A section opened up and a small square box set inside.

Tanner growled. "How did you find that? And how did I not know it was there?"

"It's spelled to recognize Royce's face." Rafe frowned and pointed at his own face. "When I stepped in front of the mirror and looked into it, I noticed that section was different than the other."

Luna took the pendent and studied it. "Royce was using dark magick the last few months of his life. He planned to kill me and my sons. That was the final straw. Because if the bastard would kill his own mate and kids, then I feared what he'd do the rest of the Pack. My Pack. I submitted fully to my wolf that day, letting her surface and take control. She'd wanted to kill Royce for a long time and I let her. I barely remember attacking him. It was like watching someone else do it."

Rafe pulled her into a hug. To Jasmine's surprise, Luna sank into his embrace. But she continued with her story and Jasmine figured she just needed to speak the words out loud. "Royce pulled a knife on me, but my wolf was too far gone. We fought for it until I knocked it out of his hand. As soon as I grabbed it, I plunged it into his heart."

Tanner tugged his mom from Rafe's embrace and held her. "You saved the Pack. You did what you had to do."

Luna laughed. "The bastard thought by giving me his Alpha power that I'd go rogue. To be honest it was a concern for me for a little while."

Hayden and Dane each placed a hand on her back. Hayden said, "We wouldn't let you."

Jasmine saw their energies—the inner power each of them carried inside—glow around them, merging. For the first time, she knew what made MoonRiver so different from other Packs and Prides. Luna shared her Alpha power with her sons. Although she was the wolf Alpha, her sons helped balance it.

After a few more moments, Luna withdrew from her sons and moved toward the door of the bedroom. She took off the necklace she wore with the tiny paw prints and put the pendant on the chain. Then she put the necklace back on. "We need to get this back to the Council of Elders to be stored in a safe place."

On the ground floor, Rhea and Alec waited for them. With their sensitive hearing, Jasmine knew they heard Luna's story. They met Luna's gaze and nodded to her before stepping outside ahead of their Alpha.

Rhea tensed and stopped, holding up her hand. Then she growled a moment before Faelin materialized a few yards ahead of them. Jasmine drew her gun while everyone else snarled and fell in a defensive stance.

Mutants like she'd never seen before stepped out from behind buildings. There must have been a dozen or two of them, surrounding them. Jasmine glanced to Dane and then Rhea and Luna, looking for a sign to either retreat or fight.

Faelin smiled at them, his features taking on an eerie, dark look. His dark gaze turned crimson and Dane cursed. "He's channeling the demon's power."

Was that how he animated the mutants to be more beast-like, instead of stuck behind human and animal forms?

Faelin glared at Luna and snarled, "Kill them."

CHAPTER FOURTEEN

Dane watched Jasmine raise her gun and shoot the mutant who charged at her. The bullet hit him between the eyes and the fucker dropped to the ground. Pride bloomed in Dane's chest, but he still worried.

Rhea moved closer to Jasmine while taunting a few mutants of her own. The female was holding back her power, but Dane could feel it building inside her. She was waiting for the right moment to strike.

Shifting his hands to claws, Dane whirled around and sliced across the chest of a mutant, then another. Kicking out, he slammed his booted foot into its chest, sending the creatures flying into a group of them. Dane drew his own gun and shot multiple rounds. He wasn't aiming for the head. He wanted to slow them down while he used the psychic connection he and the Pack leaders and the Enforcers had to call them in for backup.

Keegan was a telepath and after passing the Alpha power and title onto his eldest son, he remained in the power circle that connected the Marshals, Betas, Enforcers, and all other protectors of the Pack so they all could use his telepathy to mindlink with each other.

It was much faster than using a phone.

Something slammed into Dane's back. Pain exploded across his back and he roared and turned, connecting his fist with the mutant's jaw. The bastard stumbled back a few steps and growled before charging at Dane again.

Dane raised his gun and shot the fucker in the head. He dropped like a lead weight.

Glancing to his mom and brothers, he smirked. Luna was going through the mutants like they were deer. Tanner stuck close to her, guarding her like the sentry he was born to be.

Hayden was fighting three on his own.

A charge in the air made him spin around, ready to take on whatever just ported onto the scene. Ana and Cameron appeared. Both females raised a brow at him and he straightened. "For every one we kill two more appear. I'm not sure how he is doing it."

"A demon," Ana snarled. "I can feel the dark magick."

Cameron glanced around. "Where is Faelin?"

Leave it up to the bastard to leave a fight he started. "Fucking coward."

Ana held out her hand and a sword formed. She shared a link with Sable, who had saved Ana's life after being attacked by mutants when she was younger. The bond allowed Ana to draw from Sable's magick she possessed from being the daughter of a powerful witch.

Cameron nodded toward Jasmine. "I've got Jas's back. But Dane it'd be handy if you could turn the fuckers on themselves."

He frowned. "It doesn't always work the way I want it, but I'll try."

The supercharged empathy power allowed him to alter other's emotions. He could, in theory, send people in a rage. He couldn't control what they did after that. In fact, Dane hated the power and never learned to use it to his advantage.

But if he combined his power with Rhea's, they could end the sea of mutants. He rushed over to where the female was fighting a few of the creatures. "Can you link your power with my Empathy?"

She glanced at him and frowned. "Not sure."

She held her hands up toward the mutants and they froze in place. Dane stared at them, then asked, "Can you do that to all of them?"

"I think. I haven't explored all my abilities yet. It kind of scares me."

Her admission made him smile. She hated her gift almost as much as he did his. "Let's try together then. They just seem to be coming from nowhere."

"Yeah, I noticed." She held out her hand and he took it.

Within moments he felt her power swirled in his mind. "Fuck, that's more powerful than I imagined."

Rhea shrugged. "You push your empathy out to them all and I'll push mine out at the same time. But calm them, make them realize what they are doing is wrong. I'll use their calm states to rip their minds apart. Let's hope we get them all at the same time."

Even if they didn't get them all, the majority would be helpful.

On the count of three they pushed their power out, touching each of the minds of the mutants. That was when Dane noticed the mutants were all crazy as they believed. Their minds were blocked by something that kept them in a confused, angry state. Dane reached inside and removed that block and filled them with guilt and remorse.

Rhea pushed her Hunter's power into the mutants and started ripping their minds apart. The mutants stopped, gripped the heads in their hands, and dropped to their knees. With a final push of their magick, the mutants screamed out. Then everything fell quiet.

Dane let go of Rhea's hand and glanced around. All the mutants were dead. Jasmine walked over to him, and he tugged her into a hug.

A scream cut through the silence and he whirled around to see his Mom with a knife in her stomach. Faelin materialized behind her and wrapped an arm around her neck. He ripped the pendant from her and held it up. "Thank you two for your gifts."

Confused, Dane glanced at Rhea. She stared wide-eyed at him. "He absorbed our powers. I can't feel mine."

Dane searched within himself and she was right. Somehow Faelin had stolen their powers.

Ana cursed. "It's his connection to the mutants. As soon as you got into their minds, Faelin absorbed the magick as his own." Forming an energy ball in her hand, Ana snarled at the rogue Alpha. "Let Luna go."

Faelin laughed. "Or what?" Then he vanished, taking Luna with him.

No! The bastard took his mom. Dane howled, alerting the wolves and cats of Ashwood that their Alpha had been taken. Hayden joined with a howl of his own, then Tanner. Soon the forest filled with mournful howls.

Blaine materialized beside him. It was a protocol that if one Alpha was out of the den, the other stayed. Neither of them liked it but agreed that it was for the safety of the den. Plus it kept one of them in power in case the other was killed. A Pack without an Alpha was prey for rival Packs and rogue groups.

Blaine growled. "Rhea, take Jasmine back to the den. Everyone else hold hands. Ana I will port us to the Onyx den."

The enforcers scrambled to do as Blaine commanded. Rhea and Jasmine darted into the cave where the entrance of the tunnels were. Dane's heart ached. His mom was hurt and being held captive by a crazy fucker with a god complex.

Moments later they materialized outside the Onyx den. It was too quiet. There were no mutants to greet them. Dane stretched out his empathy and dread slammed into him. "No one is here. The den has been cleaned out."

His mom was gone.

Without a trace.

JASMINE PACED her living room while wringing her hands together. Cole and Kyle watched her from the sofa. Both their lips trembled and tears filled their eyes. They knew as soon as she entered their apartment that something was wrong.

One of their promises to each other was to never hide information. No matter how bad it was, they'd work through it. So she told them Luna was taken.

"She's strong," Kyle said.

Cole added, "They'll find her. They have to."

"I know." Jasmine stopped pacing when she sensed Dane outside her door. She rushed over and yanked it open.

His blue-green gaze locked with hers and he lunged for her, enveloping her in his arms and burying his nose into her neck. His body trembled and she squeezed him tight. After several minutes, he lifted his head and slammed the door shut. "The Onyx den was abandoned. Ana and Sable are trying to track him down. They've called in Travis, Brenna, and Byrce to help track her."

"They'll find her."

Dane framed her face and she felt the threads of the mating bond form. Mating wasn't about sex. It was about two people who belong together. The bond formed at different times, depending on the couple. Her wolf wanted the connection to Dane. If the Alpha could be taken, then so could Dane. If they were bound together, she'd be able to find him.

She kissed his lips, soft and quick. "I'm helping with the search."

He simply nodded. "Faelin took my powers."

Her wolf reached out for his and the threads started weaving together. "I'm yours as you are mine."

His eyes flashed green, then blue. He reached a hand out to the boys and they came to them instantly, standing on either side of them. Cole said, "We're a family. We will find our Alpha and bring her home. Together."

"As a Pack. As Family." Kyle added.

Jasmine nodded and locked gazes with Dane. "I love you and will fight by your side for the rest of our existence."

He hugged her and the boys. "I've always loved

you and the kiddos. I will expect all three of you at Enforcer training in the morning."

"We'll be there." The twins said at the same time.

Even though the boys were only nine, they'd train and join the junior enforcers who will say in the den to protect the Pack while the Enforcers and sentries search for Luna.

So will Jasmine.

Luna was like a second mom to her and she'd be damned if she was going to lose her to the bastard Faelin.

Shifter of Ashwood Falls

After losing over half of their dens to a group rogue shifters, the wolves and leopards merged as one Pack, but living together is much more of a challenge then they expected.

Series Reading Order
Winter Eve
A Tiger's Claim
A Mating Dance
Surrendering to the Alpha
A Rebel's Heart
Divided Loyalties
Touch of Desire
A Leopard's Path
Jaguar's Judgment
Bundles of Pink (A short story)
Shifters of Ashwood Falls Collector's Bundle
Alpha Challenge
Mating Chaos

The Collective World is filled with vampires and lycans and steamy reverse harem paranormal romances!
Please see the suggested reading order for the **Collective World** below.

Welcome to the *Collective World*

Coven's End
Kane
Voss
Quin
Jillian
The Complete Series Bundle

Academy's Rise
Hell Fire
Dark Water
Dead Air

Lucifer's War
Coming soon...

ABOUT LIA DAVIS

Lia Davis is the USA Today bestselling author of more than forty books, including her fan favorite Ashwood Falls Series.

A lifelong fan of magic, mystery, romance and adventure, Lia's novels feature compassionate alpha heroes and strong leading ladies, plenty of heat, and happily-ever-afters.

Lia makes her home in Northeast Florida where she battles hurricanes and humidity like one of her heroines.

When she's not writing, she loves to spend time with her family, travel, read, enjoy nature, and spoil her kitties.

She also loves to hear from her readers. Send her a note at lia@authorliadavis.com!

Follow Lia on Social Media

Website: http://www.authorliadavis.com/

Newsletter: http://www.subscribepage.com/authorliadavis.newsletter
Facebook author fan page: https://www.facebook.com/novelsbylia/
Facebook Fan Club: https://www.facebook.com/groups/LiaDavisFanClub/
Twitter: https://twitter.com/novelsbylia
Instagram: https://www.instagram.com/authorliadavis/
BookBub: https://www.bookbub.com/authors/lia-davis
Pinterest: http://www.pinterest.com/liadavis35/
Goodreads: http://www.goodreads.com/author/show/5829989.Lia_Davis

ALSO BY LIA DAVIS

Paranormal Series

Shifters of Ashwood Falls

Bears of Blackrock

Dragons of Ares

Gods and Dragons

Dark Scales Division (Co-written with Kerry Adrienne)

Shifting Magick Trilogy

The Divinities

Witches of Rose Lake

Coven's End (Co-written with L.A. Boruff)

Academy's Rise (Co-written with L.A. Boruff)

Singles Titles

First Contact (MM co-written with Kerry Adrienne)

Ghost in the Bottle (co-written with Kerry Adrienne)

Dragon's Web

Royal Enchantment

Marked by Darkness

His Big Bad Wolf (MM)

Their Royal Ash

Tempting the Wolf

Hexed with Sass (part of the Milly Taiden Sassy Ever After World)

Claiming Her Dragons (Part of the Milly Taiden Paranormal Dating Agency)

Contemporaries

Pleasures of the Heart Series

Single Titles

His Guarded Heart (MM)

Made in the USA
Lexington, KY
30 November 2019

57927188R00081